MW01712335

EN DUKKE

Copyright © Ellen Jensen-Dean, 2001. All rights reserved. No part of this book may be reproduced or transmitted in any form or by any means, electronic or mechanical, including photocopying, recording, or by any information storage and retrieval system, without permission in writing from the publisher.

Bedside Books
2389 South, 300 East, Salt Lake City, Utah 84115
www.american-book.com
Printed in the United States of America on acid-free paper.

En Dukke

Designed by Ben Moodie, ben@atlaswebdesign.com

Publisher's Note: This is a work of fiction. Names, characters, places, and incidents either are the product of the author's imagination or, are used fictitiously, and any resemblance to actual persons, living or dead, events, or locales is entirely coincidental.

Library of Congress Cataloging-in-Publication Data is available upon request.

ISBN 1-589-820-02-9

Jensen-Dean, Ellen, En Dukke

Special Sales

These books are available at special discounts for bulk purchases. Special editions, including personalized covers, excerpts of existing books, and corporate imprints, can be created in large quantities for special needs. For more information e-mail cln@american-book.com or call 1-800-296-1248.

En Dukke

by

Ellen Jensen-Dean

To My Danish Grandparents
for the doll
that inspired the story

Preface

Mysteries have always been my favorite literary genre so it was only natural that this became my preference in writing as well.

When I was a child, World War II was being waged in Europe. The war may have seemed far away to many children, but not to me. My grandparents were living in Denmark and contact was lost for several years while that country remained under German occupation. Watching my mother's disappointment as the mail came and went with no news from her family and friends affected me deeply.

However, a doll that my grandparents had given to me would remain with me into my adult life and eventually become a showpiece in our home.

I chose to make the role of this doll the brainteaser piece for this mystery. And because I received it just prior to the war, it seemed only appropriate that that portion of history would fit into the story which actually takes place many years later.

Chapter One

The day was so ordinary that Anna would have laughed if someone had even hinted that her family was about to be drawn into one of the most intriguing, elusive and puzzling of events; but that's exactly what her actions that day would precipitate. Had she known what was to follow, the trip to the attic would no doubt have been postponed permanently, and the resulting danger that they eventually faced could have been avoided.

Anna Hansen had been born in 1933, the same year that Adolf Hitler had become the dictator of Germany. Most of her family still lived in Denmark and referred to his rise as the "Curse of '33," for obvious reasons.

But as already alluded, there was a sequence of events about to occur. It really did all begin for Anna and her family on that hot summer day in August. California was still on daylight savings time and Anna had risen early to open the doors and windows, cooling off the main house before the stifling heat of the day could penetrate the coolness that lay within.

She had already begun closing up the house and pulling shut the drapes to further ward off the suffocating invasion of heat that would continue until sunset. The rising heat had silenced the birds that had been singing only a few moments earlier and were taking refuge in the cool shelter of the trees by the hedge. Now and then a leaf or limb would move ever so slightly, revealing a little hidden occupant.

The sprinklers had launched their morning rain over the garden, where small rainbows could be spotted, depending on the viewer's focal point. The large green lawn was a splendid showpiece thanks to Hans, the gardener. This was no ordinary lawn. The luscious green blades, so pampered and manicured, appeared as a perfectly woven green carpet edged by exotic flowers in every color imaginable.

Upstairs the children could be heard already preparing to take advantage of the few remaining days of their vacation. Like most mothers before her, Anna could not help wistfully wondering where the time had flown. She caught a glimpse of herself in the hall mirror as she passed and although the years were beginning to show, the reflection was that of a very attractive, self-assured woman. If anything, the years had added a softness that few women enjoy. Her mink-colored hair, with its natural blond highlights, curled under with no effort on her part. It lay softly in an attractive pageboy cut surrounding her delicate face. Not bad, she thought, with an amused glint in her eye. The amusement, a trait often there just below the surface, was testament to the optimistic and pleasant demeanor that was hers.

She was very proud of all three of the children, but thinking of Emelia, the oldest, being a full-grown woman was still a little scary. She was starting college this year and when she had informed her parents she wanted to major in journalism they were delighted and supportive. Anna had once aspired to that role, but when she met and fell in love with Tom, she had willingly given that up to stay home and raise a family. A decision she had not regretted.

Emelia, who greatly resembled her Danish grandmother, was tall with strawberry blond hair. The blue eyes were deep set with long lashes in a delicate face of milk white skin. Young men found her breathtaking beauty a striking contrast to her outspoken, tomboyish ways. Unlike her mother she had vowed that no man would make her give up a career. She would have both.

From the time Emelia could play with the neighborhood children, there had been a constant string of friends in and out of the house. Anna didn't mind that eventually most of the activities were focused right here. As Emelia got older, and the twins had come along, her boyfriends began to change also. Yes, Emelia was very popular. Anna could hear her upstairs, humming softly.

Well, heat or no heat, Anna still had errands to run and projects to finish before school would start again.

She could drop Cook off to do the weekly grocery shopping.

Just last week, she and Emelia had gone through some of the old boxes in the attic that had accumulated over the years. Some of the boxes still remained untouched, and most of those were the items hastily packed away when Anna's mother died three years previous.

Two boxes contained Anna's childhood things that had been sent sixteen years ago when her father had died and her mother had moved off the Minnesota farm to live with them. She had resolved to go through those boxes today and either open or close that period of her life forever.

"What's for breakfast, Mom?" It was Emelia who had come up behind her as she stood lost in thought.

"Whatever you'd like, dear, as long as it won't heat up the kitchen. The weatherman says we are in for another Southern California scorcher."

"Have J and J eaten?" The abbreviation was short for the ten-year-old twins, Jim and Joe.

"No, they haven't come down yet."

"How about if I make some pancakes for the four of us and then take them to the beach for a while?"

"Oh, Emelia, would you? I've just got to get at some of the things in the attic and I'm really in the mood for it today."

"Sounds fine to me," she said as she took off up the stairs to inform the others.

The "Oh, boy!" from upstairs verified that the plan had been overwhelmingly accepted.

By the time Anna had the first box on the floor of the attic, the children were well on their way. She cut the first string and gently opened the lid and began sorting.

There were old letters, a diary, some long outdated *Seventeen* magazines and several pieces of embroidery, even ones that had never been completed.

Suddenly, she lifted out a box with faded lettering reading, Armand Marseilles 1330. Slowly she opened the box revealing an old doll and as she did so said, "Min Dukke. My, my, the times we shared together!"

Then taking a closer look, she laughed. "You don't look so well any more, Emelia." Yes, that was the name her own grandmother had given the doll when she and her grandfather had given it to her.

Holding the doll closer, she allowed herself the luxury of drifting back in time as long-cherished memories sprang to the surface. She was four years old again, or nearly five as she would say, wanting to appear older. It was the Christmas Eve spent in Denmark that was to stand out in her memory for all time. The year was 1937 and the war still seemed far away.

She remembered it as vividly as if it were yesterday. The evening had started just after sunset and a silvery moon provided the only light as they set off in the open horse- drawn sleigh for the little white country church with its steeple reaching skyward. It lay only a couple of miles from her grandparents' cottage.

She would never forget that ride. The silence was broken by the runners of the sleigh gliding smoothly over the snow and the sound of the horses' hoofs packing the snow with each rhythmic step. There was the tinkling of the jingle bells attached to the harness of each of the two dark brown horses and the voices of the passengers that were muffled by the heavy hand-knitted scarves covering their noses and mouths.

She was seated in between her mother and grandmother in the back seat while her grandfather and father rode up front. Of course, it was grandfather who guided the horses as they jaunted along.

Snow, soft like feathered rain, continued to fall lazily on the countryside already covered with a mantle of white. The air was cool, but no breeze moved the naked limbs of the trees, adorned in their white winter coats and trimmed with crystals of smooth brittle icicles that hung like ice needles from the branches.

This had been as close to a fairyland setting as she would ever experience.

The church was decorated with wreaths and poinsettias. A pipe organ was already playing the Yuletide carols as they entered the friendly and warm house of worship. Even though it was very festive, it has hard for a little girl to sit still when she knew that before the evening was over they would be opening the presents under the tree, as was the Danish tradition.

Once back at the cottage again, it was time for the Christmas goose to be served. The table had been prepared before leaving for church and the cook had the meal ready and waiting upon their return. Anna had so wanted to skip the meal and go directly to the large living room where the decorated tree stood waiting to be lit. She was to wonder years later how they managed to keep the lit candles from catching the tree on fire, but they did.

Once the meal had been consumed they all went into the living room and, for Anna, the excitement that had steadily mounted could hardly be contained. There were more carols sung as they all joined hands and circled the tree. Then there was a Christmas story read by grandfather and finally the opening of the presents.

There were other presents, but try as she might she couldn't remember any of them except for the package with the large red bow that her grandmother handed to her.

When she opened the box she couldn't believe her eyes. Looking back at her was the most beautiful doll she had ever seen. The blue "sleep" eyes looked out of the porcelain face with its fat rosy cheeks and a rosebud mouth with diminutive teeth. The hair, real to touch, fell in long, blond curls around her face and down the back. She was dressed in a lengthy, fitted wine-colored jacket that fell softly over the long full skirt. There was a lace inset in front for the blouse. Little white cloth shoes with cardboard soles covered the feet.

She was so overcome with happiness that it had taken her a few moments before she jumped up and wrapped her arms around her grandmother's neck and kissed her full on the mouth. A little more cautious, but with the same gratitude, she went over and climbed onto grandfather's knee and kissed his cheek.

The remaining days the family spent in Denmark were a happy, carefree time for Anna. Her young age provided, though not for long, a shield from the reality of the dark cloud already forming, preparing to move across Europe.

Although World War II began in 1939 it wasn't until April 9, 1940, that the Germans invaded Denmark. She would never forget that day. She had taken Emelia and sat for a long time in her room, crying silently.

Her parents now often spoke in hushed tones whenever she was within hearing, but she picked up pieces of conversation about what they called resistance groups that blew up factories. And that helped some 7000 Danish Jews to escape into Sweden, which was neutral. Before it was over, the Germans had arrested thousands of Danes, including Jews, policemen, and, of course, the resistance fighters. They said that most were shot, tortured, or sent to prison camps in Germany.

She was so afraid for her grandparents. Would they be in any of what they called the resistance groups? Were they still alive? She would hold Emelia close, as if by doing so she could somehow transmit her love for them through her.

Then one day the letters no longer came. It would be five long years, on a cold March day, before the sad news finally came. Neither of them had survived and although they had died in their own bed it didn't soften the blow.

Emelia would remain the only link and that Christmas spent with them would stand out from all the rest in memory forever.

She quickly pushed any unpleasant thoughts away. Today was to enjoy. She held the doll up, for the first time seeing its state of disrepair. She remembered having problems keeping the arms and legs in place, but as a child she had not noticed that the doll was aging, too.

"You really are a mess!" she laughed. Then an idea struck her. Why not have her repaired? She'd make a great ornament to sit in the chair at the top of the stairs.

Once decided, she turned back to the box and again sifted through long-forgotten toys. As she went through them one by one she noted that she was repackaging more than she was discarding. Well, after all, she thought, these are the memories of a happy childhood, so why not hold onto them?

The doll was placed back in the box and moved downstairs. Yes, she did deserve to be dressed up again for all the many hours of pleasure she had bestowed on her little mistress.

By the time the children returned from the beach everything was back in its place and Anna had started supper.

"What is the ugly thing in the box? UKKK!" It was Joe who had spotted the doll that Anna had left on the TV.

"Never mind, Joe. It's just an old doll of mine I found in the attic today. I've decided to fix her up.

She'll look much better once she's cleaned up. You'll see," said Anna.

"She looks dead to me, Mom," he laughed. "She's a real mess."

"I know that she doesn't look real great right now, but just wait. Now go wash up." Anna was sorry she had left the box out in the open and wanted to end the discussion. She quickly took the box and started to shove it in the bottom of her closet.

"Don't let him upset you, Mom. He didn't mean anything by it," said Emelia, sensing that the doll was very important to her mother.

"I know. I know," she said. "I guess I'm just tired. Sometimes it is a little unsettling digging through old memories, my dear."

"I guess I don't understand what makes her so special," said Emelia wistfully.

"She's not just another doll. I had lots of them, but it is where she came from. My grandparents gave her to me."

"The ones in Denmark?"

"Yes. They, of course, could never have any idea how much she would come to mean to me. Even after all these years I feel that I owe it to them to have her refurbished. She was pretty once, believe it or not."

Emelia took a much closer look at the doll. "You know, Mom, I wonder if by any chance she's a collectable. Look at the neck," she said pointing to the back under the hairline. "There are the letters A and M plus the number 1330 engraved into the porcelain. Maybe she's more valuable than she looks." There was now a definite sparkle in her eyes.

"Valuable or not, I'm having her restored. It may seem silly, but so be it," Anna said with determination. She smiled broadly. With the final decision made, she could literally feel her spirits soaring.

"I think that's really neat, Mom," Emelia said. "I'm getting more excited about the idea by the minute."

Later that evening as Anna related the events of the day she was surprised at her husband's reaction, or lack thereof.

"Where's this doll that everybody is talking about?"

Slowly she retrieved the box, wondering if he, too, would laugh, but he didn't.

"She's not in very good shape, is she? Do you really think you can fix her, or want to? Look, the leg is even cracked."

"I know. But even fixing the hair and washing her up would help. And with a new dress and bonnet she'll be okay."

He continued to study the toy for a moment, but said nothing further. She was disappointed at his reaction, but then what had she expected? If she saw only what he saw she wouldn't be too excited either. After he had returned the toy to the box she took it and slowly put it away again in the closet. She then went to check on the children to make sure they were on their way to bed.

Long after everyone was asleep, Tom lay staring at the ceiling, listening to Anna's breathing. He could not forget the little-girl look on her face when she had shown him the doll. He was ashamed that he had not shown more enthusiasm, but he knew that the doll would need a lot more than a new dress to make it presentable.

All at once he had an idea. He would have it fixed professionally for her birthday. He had seen advertisements, in the yellow pages or some magazine, for doll repair. He would discuss it with Emelia. She could help him find someone and keep the secret.

With that resolved, he closed his eyes, moved over next to Anna and quickly fell asleep.

Chapter Two

It was a couple of weeks before Emelia and her father were finally able to get the doll out of the house without Anna's knowledge, and locate a repair shop. The shop itself Emelia had discovered quite by accident the day she registered for college. She had just come out of the parking lot, but had been unable to negotiate a left turn and was forced to go right before turning back.

It was then she saw it! In big, hand-scrawled letters the sign read, "Doll Repairs." The shop was obviously housed in the old three-story Victorian mansion in whose large projecting bay window the sign hung.

It lay snuggled behind two enormous overgrown magnolias that provided some seclusion from the street, which was perhaps why she hadn't noticed it before. It was also set back on a large expanse of lawn that appeared somewhat neglected with its five-inch growth of drying grass. The owner apparently was not overly concerned with landscaping.

Although it was an elaborately decorated Queen Anne, there were several areas on the wraparound porch where the paint was beginning to peel away. Its dark earth tone colors, however, mercifully camouflaged most of whatever decay was there.

As she sat for a moment, quickly taking it all in, her eyes saw only the beauty of the three-story turret, the ornate roof finials and crestings. She marveled at the balcony trimmed with authentic gingerbread features. In spite of its imperfections, it was a splendid example of the Victorian age of elegance, set in a more tranquil time and place.

What a stroke of luck and what a quaint setting, she thought. This is the place. Not only would it be convenient, but it was exactly what she had been looking for.

When school started, she noted the shop was open every day, but never before ten in the morning. On Wednesday, her first class wasn't until eleven so she had decided to try to take the doll then. Her dad had put it in the trunk of her car when Anna was out shopping. If Anna didn't notice it gone, so much the better. But if she did, they'd cross that bridge when they came to it. Anna hadn't mentioned the doll again.

When Emelia arrived at the shop she was pleased to see the "Open" sign in the window and the shades up. As she reached the top step and opened the door, she immediately noted the stale odor that hung in the air. It was as though she had climbed into someone's old attic.

There were dolls everywhere.

It took only a few seconds for her eyes to adjust to the dim light, most of which filtered through the heavy lace curtains draped over the leaded and beveled glass windows. The faded curtains looked as old as the house itself and had probably been installed way back then. From the outside, they served the purpose of completely obliterating any view of the inside of the house.

Even though the house was dusty, dark and cluttered, Emelia could only stare in wonderment. She had done a paper in high school on old houses, so was familiar with the architecture and charm of the Victorian homes. She recognized the Tiffany glass windows in Victorian Art Nouveau.

She noted the timeworn but still grand staircase that ascended into what she knew was the three-story turret she had seen from the outside. Over to one side was a fireplace with fresh logs already on the grate. It was apparent that this source of heat was still functional and used.

There was a magnificent, but dusty, crystal chandelier in what once would have been the dining room. There were precious antique furnishings scattered throughout, but it was clear that the dolls, which nearly covered most of them, were considered the greater treasure. It was to them that the owner devoted his or her attention and not the house.

She could hear voices coming from somewhere in the house, but could see no one. She looked around, trying to determine the best way to get their attention, when she spotted the small call bell on the counter. Tapping it lightly, she heard footsteps and soon saw a woman advancing rapidly from the back of the house.

"Good morning. I hope you haven't been waiting long. My name is Frieda. May I help you?" The words carried a heavy accent. Definitely European; maybe German.

The woman was small, probably four feet ten inches at the most, she guessed, with steel blue eyes set in the softest smiling face she had ever seen. Her hair, which was nearly silver, curled softly about her face. She almost looked like one of the dolls herself. Emelia quickly produced the doll and told her what she needed. The woman nodded at intervals, indicating that she understood.

There was, Emelia soon realized, a great difference in Frieda's assessment of the doll than theirs. She was like a surgeon doing an examination in preparation for a life-saving operation. She obviously took her work very seriously.

"Do you have the box she came in?"

"Oh yes, but it was too dusty and old to bring. I'm afraid she's lived in the attic for a very long time. Can you fix her?" Emelia asked after some time had lapsed and neither had spoken.

"Oh yes! She'll be gorgeous," Frieda said as she smiled warmly.

Emelia felt good all over. Frieda had the same expression in her eyes as Anna had had. Yes, this was the right place.

It was agreed that Emelia would check back in one month. She was careful to let Frieda know it was a surprise for her mother's birthday and that the timing was important.

When the details had been settled, she bade Frieda good-bye and hurried on to her eleven o'clock class. She felt a great sense of accomplishment. The sunshine filtering through the tree leaves added to the enchantment. She could hardly wait to share the events of the morning with Roger, who was the only other person with whom she and her father had shared the secret.

She had met Roger this past summer at a beach party. When he was introduced to her she made a mental note that the tall, suntanned blond was too handsome to be anything other than a snob and quickly wrote him off. She mixed with the others and forgot about him. As the evening wore on and the party started to wind down, small groups were congregating around the fire to keep warm. Someone pulled out a guitar and soon the group's singing could be heard far down the beach.

Emelia became aware of a pleasant baritone voice and when she turned, she looked directly at Roger, who had maneuvered his way to sit next to her.

He smiled warmly and she found that in spite of herself, she was smiling back. When the singing stopped momentarily he said, "How about a movie some time? I'd like to see you again."

"I'm kind of busy right now," she said, not wanting to get involved.

"Doing what?" he asked, unwilling to be so readily dismissed.

"Getting ready for college, for one thing."

"What college?"

Her first instinct was to just walk away, but she realized that he was just being friendly.

"Alton," she said.

"No kidding, that's where I'm at. What's your major?"

Seeing that there wasn't any way to cut the conversation without being rude she answered, "Journalism" and as an afterthought added, "What's yours?"

"I'm studying law."

Then, coming back to his original question, he asked, "So how about that movie?"

"Maybe," she said slowly.

"Do you have a phone number or do I send up a smoke signal somewhere?" he said laughingly.

By now she was laughing, too. She was beginning to think he might be rather fun after all. She was waiting for him to get out his little black book or whatever it was that he would use to write the number in, but he merely looked at her.

"Aren't you going to write it down?" she finally asked.

"No, just give it to me. I'll remember it."

She was thinking, sure you will, as she rattled it off, but to her surprise, just before he left half an hour later he said, "That was 914-8221, right?"

When she nodded yes he smiled and said, “I’ll call you.”

Maybe he’s not only handsome, but smart, too, she thought as he walked away. She tried to ignore the tingling sensation deep inside.

After the first date she had hardly let a day pass without either seeing him, or at least talking with him on the phone.

Although Anna had liked Roger, she reminded her daughter that if she wanted a career she might do well not to get serious so soon with one person.

“After all, what do you really know about him, dear?” she said.

“Well, Mom, you don’t think that I chose journalism without any experience, do you? You said yourself that I am a good investigator. Remember when Aunt Ester couldn’t find out who was stealing eggs out of the hen house? I solved that mystery in short order.

“I have interviewed Roger thoroughly. What do you want to know about him?” She laughed.

“Maybe you should check with someone other than Roger. He may only be showing his better side,” she teased.

“Oh, Mom, I have. In fact I probably have done a more thorough investigation on him than on any of my other friends,” she said.

“What does he do for a living?”

“It’s not like I am getting married to him. We’re only friends.” She didn’t add that whenever she saw him she felt her heart begin to pound a little faster. Nor did she mention the strange stirring sensation rising up in her throat whenever he touched her, something that contact with any of her other male friends had never produced.

"I know, dear, but it never hurts to know something about the background of someone you spend as much time with as you do with Roger," Anna finished.

"He is of German background. In fact, his grandparents grew up in Germany and fled the country during the war. I guess the family suffered a great deal during those years even after arriving in this country. It wasn't too popular to be German in those days. Anyway, he doesn't say too much about that part of his life.

"He decided early on to become a lawyer, which I understand delighted his family. His mother told me that since becoming a law student he spends most of his time studying. She said she was surprised to learn he'd even gone to the beach party where we met because he is always 'locked up with his books.'

"Girls have always chased him a lot, according to her, but he never gets too serious about anyone. So you see, Mom, there isn't any reason to be so concerned. We're just friends." He had made it clear that marriage was not in the cards and that fit perfectly with her current plans.

"I don't know, Emelia. For someone who studies so much, how did he get that suntanned lifeguard look?" Anna laughed.

"Well, he has been off on vacation," she came back.

Secretly Anna liked Roger a great deal, and was glad that Emelia had someone with whom to share her studies and interests, even though he was a senior and she only a freshman.

As Emelia entered her eleven o'clock class, which was English, she slid into a seat just as the bell went off. The instructor was reading off the roll when Emelia recognized a name. She smiled a quick greeting to Rudy, who was seated near the back of the room.

Rudy's dad had been their gardener for as long as she could remember. She didn't see Rudy very often any more, but when he was younger, he used to come and help his dad so Hans could also keep an eye on the boy. As he got older it was only on rare occasions, such as when his dad had been ill last winter, that he came around.

Even though they had played together as children so long ago, they had no common friends and were never close. Rudy's neighborhood was nothing like hers.

She settled down comfortably and opened her notebook. English was one of her easy subjects and as a result she rarely had any homework. Her dreams, as of today, were of one day being a world famous journalist and she spent literally hours daydreaming about it.

Chapter Three

As soon as Emelia had left the toy shop that morning, the old lady began to examine the doll more thoroughly. Suddenly she stopped, stood back and called out to her husband, Karl, who was at the back of the house.

"Karl, come here. I want to show you something."

Footsteps could be heard becoming louder and louder and soon the stooped figure of a man appeared in the doorway.

"What is it?"

"A young lady just brought it in," she said as she pointed to the doll.

He moved forward ever so slowly and began studying the doll. "Well, what of it? How soon did you promise her it would be finished?"

"Don't you see? There is something different about this one," she said with a note of mystery in her voice.

He looked again and moved closer to the doll, as if by doing so he would learn what the doll was trying to tell him.

Suddenly, his eyes widened and he pulled back sharply. He said, "It can't be! Can it?"

"I don't know," she whispered, "but we can't risk not checking it out."

It would be a month before the owner would return to pick up the doll. That should give them sufficient time and no one would ever be the wiser.

Both agreed that Karl would need help. He rushed to make a phone call, and soon he and his friend were standing ready to examine their treasure. Neither was sure if this was the infamous doll, but the right leg was cracked and it appeared that there was a piece of paper that was only visible when he pried the edges slightly apart. It was decided that he would most likely have to break most of the leg, but could he then repair it again so that it would not be noticeable?

Both held their breath as Karl fished for the paper while his partner held the opening, trying not to shatter the leg into pieces.

Slowly, ever so slowly part of the paper was removed. Disappointment flooded both of their eyes as they heard the sound of tearing paper. They needed to slow down and really figure this out before they did something they would both live to regret for the rest of their lives.

They decided to concentrate on the piece that they had been able to remove. With shaking hands, they unfolded it ever so gently and held it to the light. The edges were yellowed as evidence that the note had been hidden for many years.

The writing, to their amazement, was clear, but unfortunately it made no sense; no sense at all. In fact, it was just a bunch of numbers. Surely the part still in the leg would reveal the meaning. They had to get it out!

There was now no doubt that this had to be the long-lost doll. The owner obviously had no idea of the notoriety of the doll, nor the secrets that she contained. At least that part was in their favor. What luck! What a stroke of luck!

There was no longer any question of retrieving the remainder of the note, only how. They tried again several times, with one prying the leg apart as far as he could while the other fished, to no further avail. Not only was the remainder of the note inside, but also—they hoped—some clue to its meaning.

Finally they realized that they would need to enlist the assistance of two others. They certainly didn't want to botch this up. It was far too important.

It was nearly midnight as three men waited nervously in the dark corner of the bar. It was a secluded little dump near the college. Surely no one they knew would ever come here, so it was an ideal place.

What was only a few minutes seemed like an eternity before the fourth familiar figure entered the room. He was obviously trying to adjust his eyes to the sudden darkness that enveloped him. The man had lost no time when he heard the ominous tone in Karl's voice. The few words spoken were enough to raise the hairs on the back of his neck. He had even broken a previous engagement to come here—one that under normal circumstances he would never have considered not keeping. It was crucial that everything be handled properly and with the utmost caution. Was it possible after so many years that the scenario was still to be played out?

Why anyone would come here by choice was more than he could imagine; however, it was obviously an ideal place for this rendezvous.

Gradually the room began to take form, as his eyes became accustomed to the gloomy atmosphere. A black and white TV at the end of the bar provided the only visible light at that end of the room. Smoke hung heavy in the air, making it difficult to breathe. Although he had never been here before he could easily have predicted exactly what it looked like. To his right was the bar with what he guessed were its usual inhabitants. He chose not to concentrate on them, but began scanning the dark booths to his left and across the back of the room.

At first, he didn't see them. Suddenly, he noticed a hand motioning from the shadows of the corner booth. He walked slowly in that direction, but didn't speed his step until he recognized his friends.

He quickly slid into the booth, and as he did so, became nothing more than a blur in this isolated part of society.

"This is ideal," he said.

Soon they were deeply engrossed in what had become the common thread that would weave in and out of their lives forever from this time on.

Although Karl repaired most of the dolls with great skill and love of the work, he had never gained the proficiency to create an entire limb for a doll with this special composition body.

The friend, Otto, who had worked in a doll factory in Germany during the war years, was one of few who could reconstruct a new leg for the doll so they could destroy the original and its owner would never know the difference.

"It would not be very honest because it will certainly decrease the value of the doll. This is a very valuable doll."

"The owner doesn't even know the value of the doll and is not selling it. She is only going to use it as a decoration. What harm could it do? And the information is vital to our cause!"

"Without it we would be at the same stalemate that we have been for years. We owe it to the others."

"This has to be fate," continued Karl. "Can you even imagine the likelihood of this doll falling into our hands? It is like one in a million! If we don't take this chance, we are fools, I tell you."

"You make it sound so right, but I don't know. What if it is a trap? What if the owner really does know? But like you said, a chance like this is one in a million," Otto agreed, still hardly believing that this was "the doll."

"Don't be silly. If she did know, she would have removed the paper," said the second.

After several more exchanges, Otto agreed. "Okay, I guess you are right. Let's go for it. Now when is this doll to be picked up? How much time do I have?"

"We have it for about a month, so you'd better get started on the new extremity right away."

"I will need to see the doll so I can get to work. How are we going to do this? It won't be wise for me to be seen with either of you. Once the plan goes into effect, we cannot afford to be connected ever again."

Otto was thinking back to the night his friend had been killed. Even after all these years, he felt tremendous guilt that he had been unable to save his friend, and that, in spite of the sacrifice, the doll had been lost.

"I shall break open the leg tonight and remove the remaining paper and then I'll mail the broken parts to you. That way no one can trace it to us. Do you have a P.O. box that we can use?"

"Yes," replied Otto. "That is how I get all of my mail. There has been so much vandalism lately that I don't rely on having a box at the house."

Karl produced a scrap of paper on which the address was written, and the plan was under way. As the little group disbanded each left the booth separately and at specified intervals. All were confident that no one had seen or heard.

As Otto was driving home after the strange meeting, the doll maker's mind went back. The year had been

Chapter Three

1936. In the old doll factory in eastern Berlin, the workers had continued to turn out beautiful dolls as they had done for years. These were items exported all over the world where they would become collectors' to some, just toys to others, but nevertheless lovely to look at and be enjoyed. He had always liked his chosen profession because he knew it brought happiness to so many.

But there was an ominous atmosphere that seemed to pervade every aspect of life. Since Hitler had taken charge, he and his other Jewish friends had begun to hear stories of strange disappearances in the night. In fact, now some of them were also happening in broad daylight. It was very frightening, especially when one didn't know what these individuals were supposed to have done. How then could others avoid making the same mistakes?

It had been a cool September morning when one of the dolls had been taken to the big office upstairs, apparently for a check on the workmanship that was being turned out. They must have been pleased with the item because, as far as anyone knew, that was the last anyone saw of it. There had been some crazy story that surfaced later that the doll had been used to smuggle information out of the country. Of course, no one at the time believed that, except Otto. There were a lot more sophisticated methods that would be a lot safer and smarter. But then everyone liked to think that he or she knew something that no one else did.

It had been quite by accident that Otto had been in the adjacent room that day when two Gestapo officers had ordered the doll shipped to one Heinrich von Stubben, whom Otto recognized as a doll collector now living in England. He was well aware that Heinrich had strong ties to the Nazis and felt sure he was certainly working with them.

Otto quickly discarded the idea that the doll was for Heinrich's own collection. He overheard the officers, obviously thinking they were alone, discussing how the doll would be used in transporting an "urgent message" to their friend in England. They also laughed at how clever they were because the manufacturer would have no idea of their purpose in buying this beautiful doll.

They laughed and joked about their "perfect plan." It was apparent that they wanted to ensure that it would in no way fall into the hands of the resistance fighters. They mentioned big donors a couple of times.

Otto was just as determined that the doll would never reach its destination. From the way conversation was going, getting a hand on that list would prove helpful to the resistance. There was no way that message would get through as long as he was alive and breathing

Maybe the names on the list were even those of people they trusted and who were of great danger to their endeavors in the resistance movement. What if some of these people were infiltrating the resistance and reporting their movements back to the Gestapo? It could account for the fact that some of their attempts to assist those fleeing from the country had been discovered before the escape was complete.

Otto knew he had to leave immediately if he were to follow the officers. His feigned illness soon had him released from his job for the day. Without delay he was advancing behind them at a safe distance to avoid being detected.

After some time, they came to a large warehouse and entered with no apparent idea that anyone was watching. At first he was hesitant to follow until he recognized the building and remembered his father bringing him here as a child. It had an area where dolls were repaired and there would be a long hallway with corridors to the sides. There should be plenty of corners in which to hide should it become necessary. One thing was sure. He had to try. There was no other way for him to learn of the doll's destination.

Why would they bring a perfectly new doll to a repair shop if not to have the message hidden inside it? It was obvious that they didn't want the manufacturer, or anyone else, to know what they were doing with the doll, so no wonder they had to come here. After all, the manufacturer's alliances would most likely not have agreed with this use of the doll. The plan needed to run smoothly and this was the best course.

Once inside, Otto slowly worked his way down the hall. Seeing a stairway he went up ever so quietly. Much to his delight, once he reached the top he found himself looking down at divided spaces, but with no ceilings. He had no trouble spotting his targets and he strained to listen. The repairman, clearly one of their followers, was agreeing to open one leg of the doll, insert their message and then repair it so it would be undetectable even to a professional.

After learning all he needed to know, Otto quickly retreated down the stairs and back down the long corridor to the outside.

It wasn't until he was safely a couple of blocks away that he noticed how badly his hands and knees were shaking.

Quickly he headed to the local tavern just on the outskirts of town. From there he called one of his contacts from the movement, requesting to meet him as soon as possible. Of course, all of these conversations were spoken in such a way that, if overheard, would have been taken for just another friendly invitation.

Within forty minutes a young man in his early thirties was entering the tavern. It was apparent from his build that he was a laborer and, as Otto knew, he ran his own business. This had made it easier to leave the job in the middle of the day without having to make excuses or look suspicious.

As soon as he joined Otto, they moved to a small table near the window so their conversation would be private and they could watch the street as well. To an onlooker they appeared to be just two friends having a social drink to pass the time of day. Through agreement, they laughed periodically to add further to that scenario, although there was nothing amusing in the content of their conversation.

Otto quickly communicated what he had learned to Gerhart and when he finished, both were of the opinion that the doll needed to be intercepted.

"I agree with you; not only must there be traitors giving money and prolonging this war, but they may be actually preventing some of our people getting to freedom. We need that list!" said Gerhart with emotion.

"Then you'll help?" asked Otto, with hope in his eyes.

"Yes. I can't do otherwise," came Gerhart's swift reply. "When is the doll being sent?"

"They were promised it would go out on the six a.m. pick-up the day after tomorrow."

"You know what? I think what we should do is switch the address labels. That way there will be no missing doll and, therefore, no questions," said Gerhart.

"That's perfect. We'll write down the switched address and then go from there," Otto finished.

"Ok. This is how I see it," said Gerhart. "We'll meet some time after midnight. Let's make it one a.m. near the back entrance, and work our way to the repair area. If the doll is going to be ready for six, it will be packed and labeled before the owner goes home, don't you think?"

"Yes, we'll switch the label with another, write the new label address down and get back out before anyone is the wiser. Then all we have to do is follow the doll and figure out how to lure it away from the new owner," finished Otto.

"That should be the easiest part. Money in the right amount should solve that quickly enough."

"Ok, then I'll see you the night after next," said Otto as both men rose.

"You can count on it."

Two nights later, as Otto waited, he was grateful there wasn't even a moon. The darkness would provide the much needed cover to carry out their mission. His eyes, now accustomed to the darkness, could make out the building. There were no lights visible on the inside, indicating that everyone had gone for the night. His watch said 12:56 the last time he looked, when he had passed under a street lamp a block further back. He wasn't about to use his flashlight to check again. He knew Gerhart would be true to his word, so he waited in silence as he melted into the scenery.

He only hoped they would be able to execute their errand without any interruptions, but couldn't shake the uneasy feeling that seemed to hang over him like an oppressive cloud. He told himself to stop thinking that something would go wrong because then he might get careless and something would go wrong. He was still trying to convince himself that the plan was easy and couldn't fail when he thought he heard the sound of softly treading footsteps.

Cautiously he whispered, "Gerhart?"

"Yes, where are you?"

"Over here, next to the alley," Otto said as he stepped forward slowly. Now he could make out the shadow of his friend as they approached one another.

"Well, let's do it," said Gerhart.

The back door hung crooked and as a result the lock hadn't caught. What luck! Gerhart would have been able to jimmy the lock, but that would have taken time and undoubtedly made a lot of noise. Both were thankful that it hadn't been necessary.

Then they were inside. The long corridor lay ahead of them. Following Otto's memory and instructions, they made their way along by moving their hands on the wall.

Suddenly they stopped dead still, hearing a door creaking in the distance. They stood like statues for what seemed like an eternity, hardly daring to breathe. After what had been only minutes they decided to move on since they had not heard anything further.

"Do you think maybe we could use the flashlight so we make sure we are going into the right room?" Gerhart asked.

"I think if we are careful. No one is expecting us to be here," Otto said, hardly daring to speak.

The mist of the cool night air had penetrated the building and only added to the discomfort that both felt. Imagination was not a welcome guest at a time like this because it only conjured up visions of beings lurking in the shadows as the flashlight moved along the floor of the corridor. Neither man was easily frightened since, having worked with the resistance movement, they had built nerves of steel. Tonight, however, those same nerves were a little frayed.

"There, that should be the room straight ahead," Otto said with relief, but when he tried the door it was locked.

"Just step aside. I can spring the lock." Gerhart had no sooner spoken and the deed was done.

"Not bad," Otto said with obvious respect.

"Ok, I'll locate the doll and get at this end of things, but I think you'd better stand guard. If anyone comes back we don't want to get caught red-handed."

How like Gerhart, he thought. Always taking the hard part, but he knew he was right about someone taking up guard duty, so he moved back down the corridor to wait.

Meanwhile, Gerhart located the box addressed to Heinrich von Stubben without much difficulty. There were only ten boxes, obviously with dolls, that had been addressed and were ready to be moved in the morning.

Next he located the address labels and found that they could easily be removed and switched. He did this quickly. Then he reached for the pencil to write down the address now on the box of the infamous doll when he suddenly heard voices coming from the front of the building and bolted toward the back corridor. Otto also heard the sound and realized too late that they had mistakenly figured that if someone came it would be from the back and not the front. He was already running far ahead, believing that at any moment Gerhart would catch up. Somehow the Gestapo, probably just cruising by, had seen the flashlight in the shop and gone to check.

At the sound of gunshots Otto dashed for the alley and the only cover he could make out. He kept listening, hoping to catch the sound of Gerhart's footsteps, but the only sound was the buzzing in his ears and the pounding of his heart. He was sure it was going to rip right out of his chest.

There was still no sign of Gerhart. Oh God, please let him have gotten away, he prayed.

After what seemed like forever, he saw the lights of the German truck flash on as they were preparing to leave.

"I guess there was only one. Wonder what the stupid guy was doing anyway?" said the first.

"We'll never know. Dead men don't talk," said the second. "They just never learn, do they?"

The doors slammed shut, the engine roared, and they were gone.

Otto lay still behind the trash bin, too numb to move. He couldn't accept that it was Gerhart whom they referred to as being dead, but his brain knew better. The guilt and feeling of responsibility so overwhelmed him that when he finally stood up the wave of nausea hit him full force. He bent over and his stomach emptied in the alley.

He knew that Gerhart had had time to switch the labels. Of that he was sure, but the new address for the infamous doll was now out of reach.

He wanted to go back to get Gerhart, but he knew he couldn't risk it. The doll would never reach the intended recipient—which was part of the mission, but it could not be intercepted either. The man who may have remembered the address would never remember anything again.

As he headed home, keeping to the side streets, Otto wept for his friend as he hadn't wept since he was a child. Oh, how he hated the Gestapo and their whole rotten regime and what they were doing to his beloved Germany. He would never forget this night nor would he rest until he had revenge, even if that took the remainder of his life.

Now, driving home, Otto realized that tonight it had come full circle. Revenge at last might be within reach.

Karl hurried home and went directly to the back of the house where the doll still lay. It was only a moment before he heard the expected tapping at the door. He had not yet turned on any lights, so he fumbled for the doorknob in the half-light from the moon outside.

Then he let his friend in and closed the door behind him. As soon as the door was closed he pulled all the drapes before turning on the lights.

Now, at least, they didn't have to be concerned about breaking the leg open, but they did so very carefully so as not to disturb the remaining paper inside. After all, it was very old and fragile.

Slowly, ever so slowly, the fragment came into view. Now the leg gave way with a crackling sound under the pressure of the wedge. There before their eyes lay the priceless evidence that had remained safely hidden for so long.

Neither moved nor spoke for a few moments. It seemed almost like a sacred event to be savored for as long as possible.

Then with deliberate skill Karl began to remove the paper. There was now no longer any question that this was "the list."

They took all the pieces that had been removed and these were laid out carefully side by side. But it didn't take long to see that they still had only a part of it. They searched again. Surely, the rest had to be there, but it wasn't. After a long time, both had to acknowledge that it was not going to be as easy as they thought.

"This is in some sort of code," Karl finally said.

"That doesn't matter, my friend. I am sure, given a little time, we can figure it out. There is always logic to this sort of thing, and remember, we are living in an age of computers. We have all the time in the world now and we'll figure it out if it is the last thing we do." He was obviously trying to reassure Karl, but his own disappointment was flooding over him as well.

Chapter Four

It was Friday and all the family in the main house had evening plans that would leave the house empty. The twins were staying overnight at a friend's house. Roger and Emelia were going to the theater with her parents. Everyone was in a festive mood.

Emelia always enjoyed these events and was delighted to discover that Roger clearly did also. It was another of the many things that they had in common that made their relationship so special.

She and her parents started getting season tickets when she had joined the drama class in high school, where she managed to snag a couple of good roles in both her junior- and senior-year class plays. Tom and Anna enjoyed the plays so much and realized how they had neglected this area of their lives, one that both had relished in their dating days and prior to raising a family.

Tom parked the car in the basement parking lot under the Music Center, which included not only the two theaters presenting major Broadway hits, but restaurants and small novelty shops.

They were early, on purpose, so as to be able to wander around the area and take in the sights and sounds. That, too, was a key part of the evening.

It was the first night of the play's run here in Southern California and excitement was in the air. They were having fun watching the patrons as they milled about, exchanging greetings each time an acquaintance was spotted. There were the usual air kisses, cheek kisses and no kisses depending on the mood of the participants. There were the beautiful people and the not so beautiful people and the downright ugly people. There were the high mannered and the no mannered. The latter might have remained unnoticed except for the fact that they also tended to be the loud and obnoxious, with an apparent craving to be noticed.

Studying people in all types of dress was not only fun, but educational as well. There were the socialites dressed in evening gowns, hair with perfect coiffures that had taken several hours to achieve. There were furs and faux furs, some hard to distinguish from the real thing. They came in all lengths, in light and dark colors worn either as coats or wraps.

Although the day had been warm, as soon as the sun set, the cool night air coming in from the ocean would change the temperature dramatically in a very short period of time. Some of the patrons dressed in light clothing were apparently tourists, and were not as prepared as the locals.

There were many different ethnic groups woven into this distinctive tapestry of people, even without the tourists. Multiple cultures and professions were represented as well. It was the landscape indicative of those who had one love in common, a love of the theater.

There was the woman with the large, sparkling diamond on her ring finger, left hand. She was dressed in what was, without doubt, a blond mink knee-length coat. Although she was a real beauty, her beauty was overshadowed by her expression, one of sheer boredom. Emelia felt sorry for the handsome specimen next to her who was trying to keep her attention. I'll bet she's been pampered beyond belief, she thought. How could anyone look that bored at an event as exhilarating as this?

Anna and Tom were having soft drinks at one of the inside booths before taking their seats. They also were enjoying just roaming around and taking in the ambience of the scene. "It's just like old times, isn't it, Anna?" Tom said.

"Yes, I'm so glad we decided to do this again. I really think that Roger likes it, too," she replied.

"I'm not sure whether it's the play or our daughter that he enjoys more," he said with a smile.

Roger and Emelia wandered through some of the small shops, checking out the latest in souvenirs, although they had no intention of buying any. They would rather wait and check out those on the stand inside the theater that were associated with the play itself.

Roger recognized one of his old professors, Dr. Burke, holding the hand of a child of about six or seven, who seemed to be hanging on his every word as her eyes roamed the crowd with visible delight.

"Hi, Dr. Burke," he said. "Having a night off?"

"Yes. Oh, hi, Roger," he said, recognizing his former student. "This is my daughter, Karen. It was her sixth birthday yesterday and her mother and I promised her an evening at the theater. We have a new baby at home so my wife volunteered me as Karen's escort. Not a bad deal, huh?" he said with apparent relish.

"Hi, Karen. It looks like you're having a great time," Roger said. Then remembering his manners he said, "Oh, Dr. Burke, this is Emelia. Karen, Emelia."

"Good evening, Dr. Burke, Karen," she said as she shook his hand.

Then lowering herself to make direct eye contact with Karen said, "You are a very lucky little girl. I didn't see my first real play until I was nearly sixteen."

"Really?" She had put her hands over her mouth as she stifled a giggle. She was bursting with the thrill of it all.

"Cross my heart," she said and smiled. "You have a very charming little girl, doctor. I know you'll have a wonderful evening," she added.

"Thank you," he said. "I think it is almost show time so we'll be on our way."

"What a nice man," she said. "We should probably start heading inside, too."

"Okay, Sweetie," he said as he took her hand and they headed up the steps into the theater.

There was a young couple, just ahead of them, dressed in jeans and totally unaware of feeling out of place among those in the latest designer garb. They did have designer jeans on, so perhaps that made up for it.

"Let's check out the souvenir stand as soon as we get a program," Emelia said, reaching into her purse.

"I'm going to get that," he said pulling her hand out of her purse, and before she could protest he handed the vendor the money and took the program.

Not finding any item of interest at the souvenir stand, Roger and Emelia began to make their way along the lobby toward the staircase leading to the second level, where they would enter to their balcony seats.

They easily spotted Anna and Tom, who were already seated and enjoying some small private joke.

Once seated, Anna and Emelia in the middle with the men on the outside, Roger gave a smile of approval, saying, "These are great seats."

"Of course! What did you expect? We only go first class," she said with a smile.

Roger noted that Tom and Anna were holding hands and decided that wasn't a bad idea. Leaning over a little he reached for Emelia's hand and found it warm and soft in his. I am going to enjoy this evening, he thought as he caught her profile in his peripheral vision.

Emelia and Anna were already scanning the room to see if they might see some celebrities and soon he found that he was doing the same.

Observing a particularly attractive older couple working their way down to the orchestra seats, Emelia tapped Roger's and Anna's arms simultaneously as she whispered, "That's Lord and Lady Brewster."

"Are you sure?" Anna asked, but before receiving verification passed the word to Tom.

Following her line of vision he noted a handsome older man escorting an equally attractive older woman down the aisle. They slowly made their way, her hand all the while holding securely to his arm. His hair, which was curly white compared to her soft blond only enhanced the "beautiful people" image that they personified. Her hair, Tom decided, was probably more gray than blond, but she appeared to be someone who would use all the tools at her disposal to remain youthful in appearance for as long as humanly possible.

Tom, as most people were, was very familiar with their notoriety. Their wealth had provided them with a lifestyle that most people never even dared dream of. It was not wealth gained through hard work, but had been attained mostly due to an inheritance by Lady Brewster from her late father. They were able to live and enjoy a life that was more like royalty than even some of the royals did.

"Who's that lady over there being surrounded by autograph seekers?" Roger asked.

"I'm not sure. Do you know, Mom?" Emelia asked, looking at Anna.

"That's Charlene Chauna, the 'Cosmetic Queen,'" Tom said overhearing the question.

"How do you know that?" Anna asked in a mildly accusatory voice.

"She's been written up a few times in some of the major magazines." Now he was laughing. "You're not jealous, are you?"

"Of course not, but I'm surprised that you know that much about cosmetics," she teased.

"Actually the stories dealt pretty much with her dislike of being overwhelmed in public by fans wanting her autograph," he finished.

"Oh, I've heard of her. She is really very good looking," Emelia added. "She certainly is a walking advertisement for her cosmetics, don't you think?" she asked, looking at Roger.

Roger had already taken his cue from Tom and merely said, "I guess so."

The woman had to be in her sixties, but looking at her it was as if time had stood still. She was one of those rare women, genetically blessed, who no matter the age continued to remain youthful in appearance. It was doubtful that her cosmetics had much to do with her fresh complexion, but it could not be disputed that it was an asset to promoting her products. Products that had contributed to making her even wealthier than she already was, having been born into an affluent family.

Her raven black hair was pulled straight back into a double bun, giving her a very sophisticated, elegant look. She wore an emerald green loose-fitting dress with long sleeves coming to a point below her wrists. A dark brown fur coat was draped across the back of the chair. Her jewelry consisted merely of a ring on each hand—one adorned with a large clear stone, surely a diamond, and the other a green stone that Emelia was sure was an emerald.

Emelia was familiar with her cosmetic line even though she wouldn't have recognized the creator. She had sampled some of her fragrances, with such labels as Chauna's Eau de Jasmin and Chauna's Eau de Lavande. She had chosen the latter, but even though it was expensive had found it well worth the price.

A man in the next aisle over was holding his cell phone tightly to his ear while trying to explain to the person on the other end why he needed to break a date for later that night. Statements like, "I'm sorry, but I'm going to be later tonight than I thought. It's one of those things. I can't help that I got tied up," and "I'll call you next week, honey," could clearly be heard as he continued to present his defense. None of this seemed to faze the redhead sitting adjacent and warmly smiling at him, all the while tightly holding onto his hand.

Then the music swelled, the lights went down and the curtain went up. Thanks to a wonderful script the performers soon captivated their audience as only skilled artists can do. The play was at times both happy and sad. There was hardly a dry eye in the house as the final curtain came down.

"Wasn't that wonderful?" Anna said, looking at Tom, who only nodded and squeezed her hand.

When they returned to the house they found that all of the lights were off. It sounded like the back door slammed shut, but Tom said, "It's just the wind. I can't believe how fast it has come up, but I'll give you ten to one that's why the electricity is off. It was so calm when we left the house."

Once inside the house, he quickly located the light switch, but as he suspected nothing happened. Added to his frustration he couldn't find the flashlight. He remembered he carried a penlight in the glove compartment in the car and quickly located it. He went to the fuse box and within a short time the house was once again flooded with light.

"I am going to have to talk with J and J about playing with the flashlight and not putting it back," said Tom, who was visibly upset by the inconvenience.

After several minutes, however, the atmosphere was again relaxed. They all gathered in the living room for a light-hearted discussion about the play and some of the people they had seen. They all agreed that Lord and Lady Brewster were undoubtedly the most notable, followed closely by Charlene Chauna. The fact that the latter rarely left the seclusion of her apartment, but had attended this evening's performance, was yet another confirmation of the popularity of this particular play.

All in all it had been an exciting evening, both on and off stage.

Early the following morning the activity in the kitchen was already in full swing. Cook, who was also the general housekeeper, was making breakfast as one by one the family members appeared in the large dinging room, adjacent to the entry hall, where everyone took their meals.

Cook's name was far too hard for J and J to pronounce at an early age, so it had become just "Cook".

She lived in a small, neat apartment above the garage, but spent most of her waking hours in the main house tending to the needs of the Hansen family.

"What happened to the lights last night? I saw you running around the house with the flashlight. I thought you went to the theater." It was Aunt Julia, Tom's spinster sister, who had just come in from the east wing of the guesthouse near the rose garden.

Her hair sat upright in small tight curls above a heavily colored, bird-like face. Her appearance matched her flighty behavior. She was continuously talking to herself and often oblivious of those around her.

"We did go to the theater. It was well after eleven when I was looking for the fuse box. The wind must have knocked out something," said Tom.

"Oh, no it was earlier than that," she insisted.

Tom brushed her remark off without a second thought. Reliability as to time and events was one of Julia's weaknesses. Although she was a bit strange, she was really very lovable and no one minded having her around.

Her only true interest was birds. She read about them, talked about them, watched them and even had one in the apartment. He was a canary with a personality very much like that of his mistress. He sang constantly!

Julia belonged to the Audubon Society and any other bird group she could find in the area. This morning she was dressed for her daily bird watch near the sanctuary up in the canyon. Friends, "fellow bird lovers," would be picking her up and she was, as usual, eager to get started.

This was probably why she chose not to argue with Tom about what time she had seen the light from a flashlight. She knew it was earlier. She had looked at her clock and it was 9:10 p.m. Oh well, maybe Cook had come back for something.

"Emelia, dear," she suddenly said, "I do so wish you would come with us. You are so good at spotting our feathery little friends."

Emelia, who had on occasion taken her aunt on these trips, just didn't have the patience for this sport. She, however, did not want to hurt Julia's feelings so said with a smile, "I have my English class this morning and then some errands to run. I just can't today."

She was relieved when the older woman was called to the door by the arrival of her transport. She fluttered out the door and was gone.

As soon as breakfast was over, Cook began cleaning up. House rules were, if you want to eat, you come to the dining room. Cook had enough to do without delivering food.

She looked out the window to see Hans coming out of the gardening shed at the far end of the large green lawn. He didn't live on the premises. No one was really sure where he lived. The nice thing, Cook thought, is that he comes and does his work without a lot of talk. She didn't tolerate wasted time by herself or others.

She would clean up Julia's apartment before she came back. Even though she liked the lady, she knew she could do it faster if she did not have to listen to her constant chatter. Unlike the other household members she did not disregard all of Julia's observations. She, too, had seen the light of a flashlight and it was certainly earlier than the time stated. Maybe it was just a reflection they had both seen, but she didn't think so. It was very curious, indeed.

When she had completely cleaned Julia's apartment, she made a quick assessment of the one in the west wing overlooking the pool area. Usually unoccupied except for an occasional guest, it required only minimal attention, for which she was grateful. Now she could go to the main house and get on with the weekly cleaning there.

She knew that by the end of the week, Uncle Alfred, who was not really an uncle at all but just a very good friend of the family, would be a temporary resident of the west wing.

He was a "dear sweet old soul" sort of person. One couldn't help liking him. He was rather fun to have around, very witty and quick with responses. He had at one time aspired to become a lawyer, but something had happened, which he would not discuss even when pressed, that had changed that goal permanently. In the end, because of his extensive travels, he had become a freelance writer of books on that very subject. Needless to say, he had become an authority in that area. He seemed to have amassed a large sum of money, although there didn't seem to be much of his material in print.

Breakfast done, Emelia realized that she was running late and rushed into her English class just as the bell rang. If there was one thing that she didn't like, it was being late and feeling rushed.

She looked in Rudy's direction, but even though their eyes met he didn't acknowledge that he noticed her. He just averted his eyes and looked out the window. I wonder what is wrong with him, she thought. It seemed so unlike what she knew about him, but then he had probably changed more than she realized over the years. Strange, he had seemed glad to see her that first day.

Finally, she settled back and started to listen. She really did like English and Mr. Jones was such an interesting teacher. He couldn't be more than thirty at most, she thought. Quite an attractive man, too, and if it hadn't been for her interest in Roger she might even have considered Mr. Jones as datable material. Oh well, she smiled to herself, no need to worry about that. I have enough activities without adding a teacher to the list. After all, he was probably really dull outside of the classroom and there were at least two girls in the front row who made no secret of the fact that they were in hot pursuit of the innocent victim.

She almost laughed out loud and then realized that he was looking directly at her. Had he asked a question that she hadn't heard? She flushed slightly, but he turned and went on talking. I am not going to get caught again like that, she thought, suddenly disliking herself for being caught off guard. She really hoped that he hadn't noticed and she was embarrassed just thinking about it. However, he didn't stop or look back in her direction for some time, so finally she breathed a small sigh of relief. No one else seemed to be paying any attention to her either, so apparently it had all been her imagination. She didn't dare turn in Rudy's direction for fear that he might have read her mind, but then that would not be possible, would it? She was just being silly.

Chapter Five

It was several days later, when Anna went to pack away some of the summer clothes, that she noticed that the attic door was slightly ajar. She decided that it must have been the strong wind that was the culprit. However, when she climbed the stairs into the attic she came upon more evidence that obviously she could not attribute to the wind. Several boxes had been opened at random and the attic certainly was not the way she had left it.

When she spotted the flashlight on the floor, she had to smile in spite of herself. She would have to have a discussion with the twins. The attic had apparently been invaded by two little boys going through toys. After a quick look around, she picked up the flashlight and headed downstairs. She would clean it up another day, or, better still, enlist the assistance of J and J.

She promptly forgot about the matter and returned the flashlight to the hall closet. No wonder Tom had

had difficulty finding it when he went to look for it the other night. It didn't seem that important so she decided not to say anything to him.

Tuesday evening Emelia had decided that she would retire early. She had not felt well and with the house empty she concluded that it would be a good time to get some extra rest. She had spoken with Roger earlier and because he was studying for another exam tomorrow she knew he would not be calling later.

She looked out the window and noticed that Aunt Julia was still up. The lights were on, which was not at all unusual for her. She liked to stay up and watch the "Late Late Show."

Emelia had no sooner lain down than the telephone rang. She reached for the cordless phone at the bedside only to discover that it wasn't there. Someone, probably one of the twins, had borrowed it and failed to return it to the charger. Having no other choice, she went downstairs. But when she answered the phone, there was no response, although someone was obviously on the line. A second later, she heard a click and dial tone. She went back to bed, rather irritated by the interruption.

She was nearly asleep when she became aware that the telephone was ringing again. This time she hesitated longer before getting up and descending down the stairs. I wish we had a telephone upstairs. It would be so much easier.

When she answered it, again there was no reply. As before she felt certain that there was someone at the other end. Once more all she got was the click followed by a dial tone.

This time she found it harder to return to sleep, so she decided she would read until her parents came home.

When Tom and Anna returned, they checked in on her because they were aware that she had not been feeling well. She told them about the telephone calls.

"It's most likely a coincidence. Somebody got the wrong number and when they realized it, they just hung up. It happens all the time," said Tom. "I don't think we need to make anything out of it. Your mom and I are home now. If it rings again we'll get it, so why don't you just forget it and go to sleep? See you in the morning."

Thursday evening Emelia had showered and was getting ready to go to bed early again. This time it was because she had an early morning exam and wanted to feel rested. Like a replay of Tuesday evening, she heard the downstairs telephone ringing. She was surprised that Cook had already gone to her quarters for the evening, but decided that this time, she was not going to answer it. It's probably just a wrong number and I am just not in the mood to get up again, she thought.

It wasn't long before she was sound asleep. Not more than a half-hour later, she was awakened and felt sure that she had heard footsteps outside her door. She could feel her heart pounding loudly, not only in her chest, but in her ears as well. Finally she managed to call out, "Is that you, Mom?"

But there was no reply. She slowly went to the window and looked out on the still moonlit night, but saw nothing. There was no car in sight. By now she was enveloped in a state of panic, yet in spite of this, opened the door slightly to the hallway and called downstairs. Oh, how she hoped that someone was home.

Suddenly she froze as she heard rapid footsteps on the stairs from the attic and she remained thus as the sound continued further on down to the first floor. She could see a shadow, but could not make out what or who it might be. Next there came the sound of a chair toppling over and furniture being shoved aside as the intruder escaped out the back door.

She stood there for a moment, trembling, trying to gather her wits about her. Finally, she turned on the hall light and moved down the stairs to the telephone and called the police. She had never felt so frightened. It seemed like an eternity before they finally arrived, although it couldn't have been more than five, ten minutes at most.

"I am so glad to see you," she blurted out when she opened the door to let them in.

"Just take it easy. Are you ok?" the older of the two officers asked.

Once they were assured that she had not been harmed, they introduced themselves. "My name is Sgt. Oliver," said the one who had spoken first. "And this is my partner, Officer Davis. Why don't we sit down and you can tell us what happened. After that we will take a look around and see what we can find, ok?"

She began by telling them of being awakened abruptly by something. She didn't know exactly what the sound was, but thought that it had come from up in the attic. That it might even have been the sound of someone's footsteps, but she wasn't really sure. After she was fully awake she had this terrible feeling that there was someone in the house who did not belong there.

Just as she began to relate the part about the footsteps coming from the attic stairs, a car pulled into the driveway. It was Tom who hit the door first, on a run. His face showed alarm that Emelia had never seen before.

"What's wrong? Are you ok? What happened?" It was as if he asked all of the questions, he'd get all of the answers more quickly.

"It's all right now. Your daughter just had a real scare, but she isn't hurt. My name is Sgt. Oliver. My partner, Officer Davis, and I arrived shortly after receiving your daughter's call."

"I'm sorry. What did you say your name was again? I am afraid I wasn't listening," Tom faltered. He was so relieved to see that Emelia was obviously not harmed.

Emelia began her tale over again. Anna was by now sitting in a chair across from her with a look of deep concern. She again related how she had heard the steps on the stairs, both from the attic and then down to the first floor. How she heard furniture—she thought a chair—being pushed out of the way.

After going over each detail one more time, Sgt. Oliver suggested that they show him the house and he and Officer Davis would see what evidence they might be able to find.

It didn't take long to find the escape route that the intruder had taken. There was the chair toppled on its side that Emelia had heard. The back door was open, but strangely the lock was not broken. It looked like a key had been used.

"Maybe the door wasn't locked," ventured the sergeant.

"Oh, yes it was. I did that myself before we left. Did you open it after that for any reason, Emelia?" Tom asked.

"No, I had no reason to. I stayed upstairs. I didn't even answer the telephone when it rang. I decided after the other night I wasn't going to lose sleep over that again," said Emelia.

"What is that about a telephone call?" asked Officer Davis. Until now he had let the older man do the talking, but sensed that there might be something that they were missing.

Tom related how, on Tuesday, Emelia had been home alone and the telephone had rung twice, but that there had been no response to her hello and only a hang up. "I doubt that it has anything to do with this," he added.

"Well, you never know. Looks like someone was probably trying to establish that the house was empty and set out to burglarize it. Do you keep anything of monetary value here in the house?" asked the sergeant.

"No, we don't," said Anna. It was the first time she had spoken. She felt dazed and angry to think that someone could violate her home, her sanctuary. Worst of all, that Emelia had been here and could have been harmed or killed. What in the world would anyone think they had that would be worth the risk of getting caught for it?

"It's ok, Mom," Emelia said. She could only guess how bad she felt. Mothers, after all, were supposed to be able to protect their children at all times and at all cost. She'd never forgive herself for leaving Emelia home alone. But, of course, that was ridiculous.

The four of them continued to discuss the situation and searched the house for the next hour. In the end, it seemed pretty clear that the motive was burglary even though they could find nothing missing.

Finally, after the policemen had gone and things had settled down again, they began to take stock of the situation.

"Well, no matter what, I am going to have the locks changed," said Tom.

Emelia, who had had very little sleep, was still upset the next morning. She had just finished relating the story to Roger and was not very surprised at his reaction.

"Why didn't you call me?" Roger asked incredulously. "You could've been hurt or even worse, killed."

"I really don't think that anyone is out to hurt me. Remember, the telephone call must have been made to ensure that none of us would be at home," she said.

"I know, but you can't make assumptions, Emelia. Maybe the phone call had nothing to do with the event at all."

"I will certainly be glad when this mystery is solved," she said.

"What do you mean, 'mystery'? Is there more that you've not told me?" he asked.

"No, of course not. It is just that at times I get the strange feeling that I—we—are being watched. Sounds like my imagination is getting the better of me, doesn't it?" she finished.

"I just don't like it. Promise me that the next time you're going to be home alone, you'll call me. I'll come and stay until your parents get home. We just can't take a chance," he said gently.

She reluctantly agreed.

Chapter Six

Nearly a week had gone by since the incident and the household was gradually falling back into its routine once more.

Cook had left early to visit her sister, who was ill, so Anna decided she would do the grocery shopping herself while the children were at school. It was a task that she found much easier to accomplish alone. She didn't realize until later that she had left the roll of film at home. It was one she had promised Tom she'd have developed.

Well, she'd just finish the shopping, go home and unload the groceries, pick up the film and drop it off. It wouldn't be a problem. Actually it would make a nice little break. The day was very hot and humid and a cool drink of soda would be a real treat.

As she turned into the driveway she did not see the gardener's car, so when she entered the house she was shocked to see him halfway up the stairs.

"What are you doing?" she asked in a low voice. So low that the sound of it surprised her.

Hans was momentarily at a loss for words at being found in such an awkward position. Finally, he pulled himself together enough to mumble something about having to go to the bathroom and having the "trots." His hands were visibly shaking as he took out an old handkerchief and began to wipe his brow.

She showed him to the downstairs bathroom while he apologized over and over.

She felt sorry for the man. After all, there had been no one around for him to ask, so what else could he do? But it did puzzle her why he had not located the one on the main floor.

Anna busied herself unloading the groceries once more until he was again outside. She decided that she would forget about the film for the time being.

When she went outside for the last time, it struck a strange note when she realized that Hans had not parked his car in the usual place in front of the house, but rather a block away. Oh well, he was getting on in years, too. She could hear him cutting the hedge by the rose garden. Well, at least he always did an excellent job, and what more could one ask for these days?

That evening she casually mentioned the incident to Tom at the supper table. To her amazement his cup stopped halfway to his lips. "Would you repeat that again?" he asked.

She went through the tale once more and still could not see what had upset Tom.

"Didn't it make you wonder why he is here on a Thursday when he has done the yard on Saturday for years without fail, unless, of course, it rained?" he asked.

"No, I never gave it a thought. I guess my mind has just been so preoccupied lately with everything that has been going on that I overlook otherwise obvious things," she said apologetically.

Some time later, Tom came in from the garden with an even more puzzled look on his face. "Anna, didn't you say that Hans cut the hedge by the rose garden?"

"Well, I honestly didn't look, but that is what it sounded like. Why?"

"Come out here for a minute. Remember when I said a week ago that the hedge was looking a little scraggy and that it needed trimming?"

"Yes," said Anna.

"Well, take a look at it and tell me what you see," he said.

"I can't believe it! I know what I heard was the hedge cutter. Maybe he cut only on the other side and will finish it on his next visit," she ventured.

"No, I wondered that myself, but I checked it out and nothing has been cut. Nothing!"

"What can it possibly mean? You don't think he has gone over the edge, do you?" she asked in disbelief. "To be sure he didn't look too well this morning. He was shaking and pale and he was perspiring profusely.

Maybe he just got the days mixed up. Let's not say anything to anyone. We certainly don't want to cause him any undue embarrassment, especially if there is a logical explanation."

So it was decided that the matter be dropped, at least for the present time.

Emelia happened to notice that Rudy was not in his seat in class. Funny, she thought, I wonder if he is sick or something. He missed class last week a couple of days, too. If he continued to do that, he wouldn't be able to get credit.

She had overheard her mother and father discussing something about Hans, but when she asked what it was all about, they merely said that it wasn't anything important and they wouldn't elaborate. Still she had already heard part of the exchange. It was apparent that Hans had been found wandering in the house looking for the bathroom. She really thought that strange, especially since she remembered that he was the one to whom Cook had turned for help one morning, about two months ago, when the downstairs toilet was threatening to run over. How could he possibly have forgotten where it was?

Maybe he was becoming senile. Maybe that was what was bothering Rudy, who probably thought that everyone was aware of the situation. Things had certainly been awfully complicated lately. So many unusual things taking place—or maybe it was just the full moon.

Chapter Seven

The following day Uncle Alfred arrived as usual with all the pomp and ceremony of a potentate. He was clad in the latest fashion offset by a magnificent tan that made him appear a great deal younger than he really was. Still very handsome, he continued to charm the ladies with flowers and lavish attention or whatever seemed necessary at the moment to maintain his debonair status. It was an expensive art form for him, but one that he enjoyed tremendously.

It was rumored that he had, on one occasion, challenged a young suitor when the two of them became stinking drunk. The young man's mistake had been his failure to recognize that the object of his affection was Alfred's current romance. Alfred loved to drink, but it was, indeed, a rare occasion when he was drunk. He could hold his liquor well.

The only dark part about this delightful trip west was that he had once again begun having nightmares about the "war years." He thought that he had surely left all this behind when he retired. He didn't have any information for them now. He thought he had made that very clear the last time they had one of those secretive trysts. Would he never be free? What was there to gain now? It was all so long ago, but still maybe the goal of the "assignment" had not yet been fulfilled.

He could still vividly remember, as though it were yesterday, the stranger who had arrived at the small hotel outside of London and registered for the night. The man instructed the desk clerk that he was expecting a message within a day or two and would be staying only until its arrival. The desk clerk might have thought this a little strange, but then there were a lot of strange things going on during the war years, what with people coming and going constantly. There were daily reports and rumors of the possibility of war that might involve the British themselves.

The stranger was given a room and directions to the eating area. He didn't reappear again that evening as far as Alfred could remember.

The message, in the form of a large package, arrived early the next morning and because the clerk knew that the guest was eagerly anticipating its arrival, he rang up the room at a little after eight. The man, who was blond and blue-eyed, and rather handsome in a rugged sort of way, came down quickly, picked up the package and went directly back to his room.

What the clerk did not know was that the package contained a beautiful doll. However, Alfred, who had also been at the same hotel, did know. Plus, he knew that in one of its legs was a hidden message meant for the recipient only. When Alfred saw the man emerge from the room, he noted that he was pale and panic-stricken. He muttered something about it being the "wrong doll" and "I must catch a plane back to Germany right away."

What could possibly have gone wrong? The wrong doll had obviously been sent, but where in the world could the original one be? If it were to be intercepted and fall into the wrong hands it would be disastrous, not just for the stranger, but for others as well.

The stranger checked out and was gone. He never did reach Germany, or even the airport. A car had come out of nowhere as he rounded the corner on foot, and he was killed instantly. The car had vanished as quickly as it had come.

Alfred had stayed on to follow the police investigation. He breathed a sigh of relief when it finally netted nothing and the death was ruled as accidental. One of the officers commented that the doll, which was strewn over a large area, must have been a gift for someone the man was en route to visit, perhaps even his child. When there was no response to ads in the paper, the case was closed forever.

As the years passed he had nearly forgotten about the doll. He had no way of knowing that the past was about to catch up with him. Now retired, his immediate thought was of spending a most promising and delightful vacation with his friends here in California.

Only when his suitcases, which appeared to be sufficient for an extended world tour, had been deposited safely in the West Wing, did Alfred set about comfortably settling in. He did not surface again until dinner was served at six.

As usual, Alfred was right on time. He did not believe in being late because he felt very strongly that tardiness was a major flaw and, of course, he had no flaws.

Cook welcomed him warmly and invited him to sit at the head of the table opposite Tom. This was designated as the place of honor whenever a guest of his stature arrived. He smiled at her and said, "I have so looked forward to consuming some of your delicious recipes. Traveling as I do, it is rare to find someone who is able to delight the palate as you do." With this, he made a small bow in her direction.

She flushed and began to giggle. Although she knew that Alfred was a lot of talk, she nonetheless enjoyed the compliment because she felt that it was well deserved.

"You are just too kind," she said and determined that she would make his favorite dessert within the week. He loved flaming cherries jubilee and although it was an extra amount of work, for him it would be done.

"Hi there, Old Boy," he said as he held out his hand to Tom, who had just entered the room. "Sure is good to be back in California again and able to stay in such comfortable accommodations. This is so much better than a hotel, and that goes for the most luxurious of them."

"We are glad to have you, Alfred," said Tom, who sincerely did enjoy having him around. He was always in a jolly mood and full of stories from all over the world. There was nothing dull or boring about Alfred. "Won't you make yourself comfortable. Anna will be down in just a moment. She just went to freshen up a bit."

"I hope you don't mind, but we've invited Uncle Frederick and Aunt Joanna to join us. When they heard you were coming to the West Coast they insisted they wanted to be here to welcome you. They should be here any minute, but Joanna isn't any more organized than ever. Poor darling has been so pampered that one wonders what would happen to her if she didn't have Frederick."

Alfred didn't say anything, but he was inwardly very annoyed at the tardiness of the other relatives. Unlike Alfred, Uncle Frederick and Joanna were relatives. Frederick was Anna's father's brother. Alfred also let pass Tom's remark about poor Joanna. He had no doubt that this woman was shrewd and well able to care for herself, although she was always whimpering about something and made sure she was waited upon hand and foot. In fact, behind all of that makeup, he saw a very hard and determined woman with no evidence of any gentleness or kindness. He rather wished that she were not coming. There was something about her that made him very uneasy, almost as though she were able to read through him. He didn't like it at all, but he must make the best of it. He certainly didn't want to offend his host and hostess, and after all, it would only be for the evening.

Suddenly a car was heard arriving out front and Tom rushed to greet the couple. As usual, Joanna sat stiffly in the car until Frederick hurriedly opened her door. She smiled as soon as she saw Tom coming down the sidewalk. She liked Tom and had often remarked that Anna had really gotten a plum when she married him.

By the time that they were in the house, Anna had come down and was simultaneously welcoming them as well as Alfred again. The twins were already standing next to the table and eager to get to the food. Emelia was helping Cook with the finishing touches on the table, and before the greetings were done, the meal was ready to be served.

"It is so good to see you again, Alfred," Joanna gushed. "We were so honored when Anna called and asked if we could join them in welcoming you. What brings you back to these parts, other than the excellent company?" she finished.

"Actually, it is a combination of business and pleasure," he said. "The timing was just perfect for both." He didn't volunteer any more and she was obviously disappointed, but didn't press him further.

Chapter Eight

Anna reached into the bottom of the closet and a box tumbled on its side. As she went to replace it she noticed that it was the doll box and it was empty! A small round curved piece of cardboard was all that was left inside. She was about to replace the box when she noticed the part. This was the hard curved piece of cardboard that covered the opening in the ceramic head.

Where was the doll? Someone must be playing a trick on her. Well, she wasn't going to let on that she was aware of the missing doll and would let the little prankster or pranksters play out their game. They were obviously expecting some reaction from her, but she wasn't going to say anything. Where do you suppose they have hidden it, she wondered?

She had just replaced the box, and when she turned around there were the twins. She smiled at them and said, "What are the two of you up to now?"

She suddenly remembered the disarray in the attic and decided it was time to confront them. When she had finished her account of going to the attic the day after the windstorm and finding the flashlight on the floor of the attic, she paused to let them give their account.

Both just stood there with looks of innocence. It was Joe who spoke first. "What are you talking about, Mom? We haven't been in the attic since you straightened it up the day we went to the beach with Emelia."

"Of course you have. The place looked like some little boys had a field day going through the toy boxes."

"No, honest, Mom. Joe is telling the truth," Jim piped up. "We wouldn't do that after you had just spent so much time getting things in order. And besides, many of those things are yours anyway. Why would we be going through that? Plus we wouldn't need a flashlight. There is already a light up there which is much brighter than any old flashlight."

Anna was taken aback. What could possibly have made such a mess? Or rather, who? She would have a word with Cook. After all, she was in the house more than anybody and if someone had been up there she would most likely know who it had been. There had to be a reasonable explanation, but what could it possibly be?

Chapter Nine

With the end of daylight savings time, the days now seemed too short. Emelia preferred sunshine and would have liked for the summer to last longer. Twilight was coming earlier and earlier each day as summer drifted lazily into fall. It was now near the end of September and the days were hot and stifling in California.

It was the Friday before Anna's birthday as Emelia maneuvered her car down the side street by the college to finally pick up the doll. She could already feel her excitement mounting as she rounded the corner and saw the now familiar sign, "Doll Repairs."

She had confiscated the box that the doll had "lived in" for so many years, cleaned it up and it was now perched neatly on the seat next to her, awaiting its occupant's return.

She was silently complimenting herself on what a great job she had done on the container. She was proud, to say the least, that the end result was worthy of notice.

Even her father had remarked about it when she showed it to him the evening before.

What she had not shared with her father was that when she had first taken the box to clean it, she discovered that the hard curved piece of cardboard, the covering to the opening in the ceramic head, was still in the box. She wondered how she could have missed it when she removed the doll. She had been about to put it aside when she noticed that there seemed to be a piece of paper with old faded numbers sticking out of what apparently were two divided parts of the wig dome.

"I wonder what this is?" she asked out loud. The numbers seemed to be like serial numbers in long strings.

Finally she decided it was probably just wastepaper that had gotten into the printing process and then become caught in the dome. She had set the paper aside and then turned back to the box. At first she was concerned that by cleaning it, the lettering might come off. Instead, it had remained not only intact, but almost looked more vivid than before she started. She was glad now that she had not replaced the box, which she had originally intended to do. She had remembered reading or hearing somewhere that a doll's value is increased if it is still in the original box. It had, however, taken her several days to work up the courage to start the project because she didn't want to spoil anything.

She had worked slowly and deliberately to preserve as much as she could. Once completed, she had been amazed at how very unique and well preserved the container really was. The lettering had hardly faded at all. It was now obvious that the doll had not spent much time in it during Anna's childhood. When the doll had been returned to the box many years later with loving care for safekeeping, the box had received the same respectful treatment.

Emelia kept the box in her own closet once she had begun its renovation. Anna had apparently not noticed that it was gone because no comment was ever made. So far, the plan was going even better than either she or Tom had anticipated.

Finally, the long-awaited time had arrived. Emelia was so pleased to learn that the doll was ready for her to pick up, because she would now have time to get her home, wrapped and put away so that her mother would be surprised in the proper fashion. Here she had worried for nothing, thinking that the repairs would be delayed. What a relief, she thought as she pulled up in front of the shop. She picked up the box next to her, again admiring its antique quality.

Emelia opened the car door, handling the box carefully. She almost laughed to herself, thinking how the valuable item had been sitting unappreciated for so long on a shelf in the attic and now that it had been cleaned up it was treated like a priceless jewel.

Once at the top of the stairs she opened the door. The stale smell was just as pungent as she remembered from her previous visit, but this time it seemed more unpleasant to her. It took only a moment or so for her eyes to adjust to the soft warm glow of the room that seemed to more than compensate for the smell.

"Welcome, my dear. I have been expecting you," said Frieda. "When you called yesterday I was afraid we would not have the doll completed, but I stayed up last night. I knew that you wanted it for your mother's birthday."

"I really do appreciate that," said Emelia. She really did like the older woman, who reminded her of her own grandmother.

"She is absolutely beautiful. I'll go get her for you," said the older woman.

As she retreated to the back room again she looked almost angelic as the light surrounded her head like a halo.

Emelia could feel the excitement mounting within her. She placed the box on the only vacant area she could find on the table in front of her.

Soon Frieda was back, carrying the priceless toy. Emelia could hardly believe the transformation that had taken place. It was no longer a dirty, tattered old doll. In its place was a princess-like image dressed in velvet, silk and lace, the likes of which Emelia had never seen

"Oh, my. What a magnificent job you have done! Mother will be delighted. She is gorgeous. I know she will be just speechless," interjected Emelia.

"How much do I owe you?" asked Emelia after a few moments.

"$125 should cover it," said Frieda.

"That sounds more than fair. Are you sure?" said Emelia, as she began to place the doll in the tissue-lined box.

As she pulled the paper over the first side of the doll, Frieda suddenly reached to help her.

"Is this the original box?" asked Frieda carefully.

"Yes, it is. I did a pretty good job cleaning it up, don't you think? I was afraid I might ruin it, but it was easier than I thought it would be."

By now Frieda's eyes were glued to the numbers and letters on the box. Could this hold the clue that they so desperately needed to unravel their list?

"Could you wait here for just a moment?" asked Frieda. She was obviously alarmed about something. All of a sudden, Emelia had a very strange feeling that something was very wrong. She had had this same feeling a couple of times in the past and, unfortunately, she had never been mistaken.

"No, I really must be going," she said. "I have an appointment and I have to be on time."

She was grateful that she had brought cash with her so that she would not have to spend time writing out a check. She quickly counted out the money and handed it to the woman. Just as rapidly, she finished wrapping the doll in the tissue paper, put on the lid and began to leave.

Something was definitely wrong. Now as she looked around the room to leave, not only did she feel Frieda's eyes on her, but it also seemed as if the eyes of all the dolls around the room had come to life and were also looking at her. She had to get out. She couldn't breathe.

Chapter Ten

Once outside and safely in her car, Emelia drew a deep breath. Her heart was pounding loudly in her ears. What in the world is wrong with me, she wondered. But still the feeling persisted. It was now nearly dark, which only added to the atmosphere of imminent danger that seemed to be all around her. She instinctively locked the doors and started the engine. She visualized the car not starting, like in a bad dream, but it turned over instantly. She pulled away from the curb and accelerated so quickly that she nearly ran a stoplight a block away.

As soon as she had left the shop, Frieda was on the telephone. She was almost hysterical and the party at the other end of the line was having great difficulty in understanding her. Finally, Karl was able to decipher that when the doll had been picked up there was a box that contained numbers and letters that might hold the answer to their list.

"How long ago did she leave? What kind of car does she drive?" he asked hurriedly.

"I am not sure. It is one of those little sports cars. It is blue. Oh, and I do remember her license. It is one of those cute ones. It says 'Emelia' on it."

"Good. Don't go anywhere in case I need for you to get in touch with any of the others. I am going to call someone right away." His voice trailed off and she realized that he had hung up.

It didn't take Karl long to make contact with his partner. He had a pretty good idea where he might catch up with Emelia, although he still wasn't sure what he would do once he got to her.

When Emelia was finally a couple miles away, she began to lose the ominous feeling that had hung over her. She breathed a sigh of relief. It was then that she noticed the lights in her rear view mirror coming closer and closer at a very rapid speed.

My goodness, that guy is going to run into somebody if he doesn't watch what he is doing. He must be drunk! She said to herself.

Just when she thought he was about to pass her, the car slowed and moved in directly behind her. She turned a couple of blocks later. So did the car behind her. It must be just coincidence, she thought, but decided she would turn again. As she did so, the same thing happened again. The car followed her.

She was within a mile of Roger's house before she was able to really comprehend what was happening, although she had no idea why. If she were to speed up—and her little car could outrun almost anything, according to Roger—she might be able to lose them by taking the back way to his place.

"Well, here goes," she said, and stepped on the gas.

The engine roared and she was off. The distance at first between the two cars increased greatly until the other realized what she was doing. Soon the distance was again closing in, but by now, Emelia was so determined that she found she had regained her nerve. First she turned right, and left and doubled back. She turned off her lights, realizing that she was not only putting herself in real danger, but anyone else who might come across her path.

Finally she stopped the car entirely and waited in the darkness of a side street. She saw the car pass. It was a black Oldsmobile like the one she had seen parked in the driveway of the doll repair shop the first day she had gone there. But this is crazy, she thought. What in the world could they want from me?

It just didn't make any sense. She sat in the darkness for nearly half an hour and when she didn't see any further sign of the car decided she would go to Roger's. She hoped that he would be home.

When she rounded the corner she was relieved to see his car in the driveway and lights on in the house. She pulled in directly behind it and began to get out. On second thought, I'd better take the doll with me, she decided. She didn't know what was going on, but it may have something to do with the doll.

With the box under her arm, she hurried up the steps and rang the doorbell. Within seconds she could hear his footsteps coming down the hall.

"Come on in. What a pleasant surprise," he said, but suddenly stopped when he saw her pallid face and frightened eyes. This was not like her at all.

"What's wrong?" he demanded.

She fell into his arms. "Oh, Roger, I have no idea what's going on. I was followed by a black Oldsmobile that nearly ran me off the road. I haven't got a clue what they want from me."

She went on to tell him about the trip to the shop and that she had been followed after she picked up the doll. Also how the car that had pursued her—because she was sure that was exactly what had happened—was just like the one she had seen at the repair shop on another occasion.

"I can't believe it!" said Roger when she had completed the story. "Why do you suppose anyone would want to harm you? It seems so meaningless."

"I know. I just can't figure it out. It was like one minute everything was fine and the next I had this awful feeling that something terrible was going to happen. Frieda changed so suddenly and I have no idea why. This whole thing is just getting so crazy. Am I losing it, Roger?"

"Of course not, Sweetie. Someone doesn't just follow you like that without a reason. Particularly when it isn't someone you know. Of course, Frieda could have called someone, I guess, but why?" he finished.

"Maybe we'll never know. I just hope it's over," Emelia said without conviction.

"Well, you're not driving home by yourself," said Roger. "We'll wait another hour and then I'll follow you home. That way, if the nut is still out there, he'll give up and go home. I just don't want him to know where you live. By tomorrow the whole thing should blow over. At least, I sure hope so."

After the hour had passed and no strange vehicles had been sighted in the neighborhood, they set out for her house. The drive, as hoped for, went uneventfully and she was safely deposited at home.

After relating the events to her parents, Tom was ready to call the police. "There is something awfully strange about all this," he said. "I am not one to jump to conclusions, but this is too strange to be coincidental."

He tried to push the thought from his mind that perhaps all the strange events of this summer were not just coincidental. Maybe they all fit together in some weird way. He didn't share his concern with anyone, but made a mental note to check with one of his friends on the force in the morning. No need to worry the others if it just turned out to be nothing.

At breakfast the next morning, the story was shared again with Julia and Uncle Alfred, who were all ears.

"That's why most of my friends are birds," said Julia. "At least, they don't drive you crazy. There are some awfully funny folks out there."

The twins fought to keep from laughing. They loved Aunt Julia, but for her to call other folks funny was almost too much for them,

As for Uncle Alfred, his interest was really piqued. He kept asking Emelia questions. She was his favorite "niece" and it was apparent that the thought that someone would harm her made him angry.

Of course, not all of the story had been told to the group, only the part about the car chase. After all, the part about the doll repair shop could not be shared or Anna would know about the birthday surprise. It made it doubly hard for Emelia to concentrate on the events as she was questioned without giving the secret away.

Eventually everyone, to Emelia's relief, decided it was most likely an isolated incident.

Chapter Eleven

It seemed that everyone except Roger had bought into the idea that the car chase had been an isolated incident. He did not want to upset Emelia any further, but there seemed to be something very mysterious happening ever since the doll had been taken to the repair shop.

The intruder a couple of weeks ago, the unanswered telephone calls, and now the chase from the shop itself once she had retrieved the doll. Was it possible that some dark—perhaps even deadly—secret was attached to the outwardly beautiful doll?

He shuddered at the thought that something awful could have happened to Emelia. He had to get to the bottom of this and end whatever the nightmare was that seemed to be evolving. He determined that he would discuss it with Tom at the earliest moment, when they were alone, even though he still had no idea what the secret might be. If there was, indeed, a secret attached to the doll, was it possible that someone connected with the repair shop had inaccurately deduced that Emelia had also discovered it? He decided she needed to be alerted even if there was only the remotest possibility that she might be in mortal danger.

This was really bizarre. I must be losing it, he thought. Isn't that what Emelia had said last night? How in the world can a doll given to a small child so many years ago have any relevance today? And why in all the years that Anna had owned it had no one gone after her nor the doll until now? It had certainly not been concealed in any way.

He just didn't know what to think, but his intuition would not let go of the idea that it was all linked to the doll. How could he prove something when he didn't even know what he was trying to prove?

After much soul searching, later that evening Roger did decide to confide in her about his suspicions.

"Is there anything at all you haven't told me, anything Frieda might have said that you didn't think was important?"

"No. Wait. There was one thing. Her demeanor didn't change until I started to put Emelia into the box. She seemed to be trying to hold her back or maybe—yes, that's it! She was very interested in the box. She may have been holding the paper aside to look at the interior of the box.

"I had just told her how I had tried to restore it to its original appearance and she hung on my every word. What do you suppose that means?" she asked.

"Was there anything unusual about the box? I mean you did spend a lot of time when you cleaned it. Do the numbers and letters make any sense in Danish?"

All of a sudden Emelia sprang to her feet.

"Where did I put it? Where could I have put it?" Her eyes were wide with excitement.

"What are you talking about? Put what?" He was now on his feet also.

"When I went to clean the box, I found that I had left the wig dome in the box." she said.

"What is a wig dome?" he asked, before she could go on.

"It's the curved piece of cardboard that covers the opening on top of the doll's head. The opening provides access to put in the eyes etc., but once that is done the dome is put in place before the wig is put on. Without it, the top of the head would collapse."

"So? What about the dome?"

"Well, when I picked it up I noticed that there was a small piece of paper wedged in the dome. It contained numbers that looked like a long string of serial numbers. I thought it was just wastepaper so I put it aside. Now, let me think. Oh, what did I do with it? I was in the sewing room at the time. I think I just laid it down on the bookcase." The words came tumbling out in rapid succession.

"Let's go, Sweetie," he said as he pulled her by the arm.

"Oh, how could I have been so stupid? I'll bet it's gone. I sure hope Cook didn't clean the room early. She usually leaves it until Saturday."

A quick search of the room revealed nothing. They were about to give up when Emelia burst forth, "There it is! There it is!" Lying wedged up next to the sewing basket was the precious item for which they had been looking.

"Don't get too excited, yet. After all, this may not mean anything at all."

He carefully opened the small scrap of paper and saw what she had seen, a paper with numbers and nothing more. At first, he looked a little disappointed, but quickly brightened. It is probably a code, but to what? And if it is, how could it possibly have any value after all these years?

"We have a mystery to solve, and if I am not wrong someone wants this little scrap of paper very badly. We must be very careful, do you understand?"

She nodded her head, slowly letting the implication sink in. She was beginning to feel the danger again. It was both frightening and exhilarating at the same time.

Chapter Twelve

Anna's birthday party was one of the best-kept secrets in the Hansen family. Not even the twins had leaked it and for them this was a real feat.

Cook had the details down pat and the cake was one of her superb creations. Anna figured that there would be the annual cake, but had no idea of anything else and suspected nothing.

Tom, as Emelia had been, was very pleased with the results of the doll. Even though he admitted he was not a connoisseur of dolls, this one had to be the best. He knew that Anna would be delighted. He didn't have to feel guilty any longer for not paying more attention to her when she had first shared the doll with him. He was very pleased with himself and Emelia. They had really outdone themselves this time.

Uncle Alfred and Aunt Julia were, of course, going to share in the family party. This was one of the advantages of being on the premises at the right time. Julia loved parties and nothing could have kept her away. She was just glad that Uncle Frederick and Aunt Joanna were not invited. This was, after all, a small family affair.

Cook had served a wonderful meal and now everyone was ready for cake and then the gifts. Anna had been so surprised that she had been kept in the dark so successfully. "I can't believe you were able to accomplish all of this without my knowledge. There goes my theory that I am the only one who knows everything that is going on," she laughed. It was an amused, happy laugh.

Tom looked over at his wife and winked. It was in moments like this that he felt so very lucky to have her as his wife. He had never regretted the day he had asked her to be his bride. He knew he never would. He was more than a little excited when he thought about what her reaction would be when she saw the doll.

Finally the time came to open presents. First the twins gave their mother a big hug, wished her happy birthday and presented her with two tickets to see "Phantom of the Opera," which was due in town next month. They had saved their allowances and done odd jobs around the neighborhood to be able to save up enough money.

Anna knew that it had taken a lot of work for them to come up with such a special and thoughtful gift. "And you can take anyone you want, Mom," laughed Joe. His brother quickly agreed.

"Maybe I'll take your dad," she laughed. "My other beaus aren't special enough."

"There better not be any other beaus," said Tom, eyes filled with amusement.

"Now it is time for a special gift, Mom. This one took a lot of family cooperation to pull it off."

"Just close your eyes, my dear, and don't open them until we tell you," instructed Tom.

She kept her eyes tightly shut even as she sensed people moving about. She could only suppose this meant that they were bringing the gift into the room, whatever it might be. Try as she could, she didn't have a clue what was going on.

"Ok, open your eyes."

In front of her was a package wrapped in beautiful flowered paper with a white ribbon and one large pink rose.

"It is too lovely to open," she said softly.

Slowly she loosened the ribbon and removed the rose, which she handed to Emelia with the instructions "Please put it in water. It is so lovely."

Now the room was quiet as all eyes were on her. The outside paper fell lightly to the floor as she held onto the box. Her expression gave no indication of what she was thinking. She looked at the box, obviously aware of where it had come from. She continued to hold the box for a moment longer before she finally lifted the lid.

"Oh," was all she could say when she realized what the present was.

"Min Dukke," she said with tears in her eyes. She gently lifted Emelia out of the box and was overcome by the magnificent change she saw before her.

The hair had been shampooed and neatly reset to its former coiffure. The bonnet had been lost long ago, but now a new one graced the beautiful head. Obviously the person who had renovated the doll had been very familiar with the style because it looked like a replica of the original. It was perfectly fitted to her head, with the typical half brim around the front and long wine-colored tie ribbons, all of which matched the color of the dress. And just as Anna remembered there was the small off-white ribbon rose on the inside front of the brim. It, like the original, was lined in silk of the same color. It looked very elegant.

Her outfit, similar to the old velvet jacket over the long full skirt, had been painstakingly duplicated as to style and cut in the new fabric. The pantaloons of white lace reached her shoes, which were once again white with new laces.

The rosebud mouth now revealed more sharply the whitened diminutive teeth. She looked as though at any moment she might speak. Her petite eyebrows had been faintly retouched in brown. Beneath them, the blue eyes retained their original color and lifelike quality of following the movements of the viewer. All of her features had been so meticulously restored that to say she was beautiful was an exaggerated understatement. She was magnificent.

"Oh, she is more lovely than she has ever been. How can I ever thank you? When did you decide to do this?" The questions continued to spill out. And so, between Tom and Emelia, the story was unraveled for her.

Uncle Alfred, as before, was very interested in Emelia's story about how she was chased, but now there was an even more ugly twist to it.

"It may have something to do with the doll." He said it almost as though he were speaking to himself.

Roger could feel the hair rise on the back of his neck.

"Please let me see her, Anna. She is a very unusual doll, isn't she?" Alfred asked. "How old were you when you got her?"

"I was nearly five. She was made in Germany, but my grandparents gave her to me as a Christmas present. It was 1937, I believe," said Anna.

He seemed to be studying the doll with a great deal of interest. Perhaps he knew of her value. After all, he was well read and well traveled. He was interested in many things that most men would find very boring. If there was one thing he was not, it was a one-faceted man.

"Well, what do you think, Alfred? Did we get our money's worth?" interrupted Tom.

"You certainly did! This is a real treasure. I would be very careful with her," he said looking at Anna. "This kind of doll comes only once in a lifetime. Perhaps that is what the toy repairman may have realized a little too late and merely wanted to buy her back. But then, I guess we will never know. It pays to be careful," he ended.

Emelia thought she detected a different tone in Alfred's voice. What did he mean by "It pays to be careful"? She pushed the thought aside as soon as she looked over and saw how extremely happy her mother was. Her father had his arm around her and kissed her gently on the cheek. She hoped that when she got married, she would find the happiness that her parents obviously shared. Seeing them like that made her feel so warm and secure.

Suddenly she looked across the room and Roger's eyes met hers. He smiled that sweet smile of his. He really does fit in well here, she thought. She had so much to be thankful to him for also. He was strong like her father, reliable, trustworthy and she really liked being with him. Maybe someday…but for now she wanted things to stay as they were, status quo.

Why was Alfred still studying the doll? He was checking the clothing, the shoes, and the hair. She had never seen anyone, other than Frieda, so interested in the doll. Of course, she could not have known that he was thinking back to another time, another place, but maybe not another doll.

"Oh, dear, I knew I'd drop it." It was Julia's anguished remark that put everyone's attention on her.

"It's my earring. My mum gave it to me. I always try to make sure that the back is on securely because I know I can never replace it."

She seemed terribly upset and was already scanning the floor around her chair.

"Don't move, Julia," said Tom. "We'll find it in no time."

He thought it better to keep the lady seated because after all, with her eyesight it was very doubtful she'd be of any help at all.

After several minutes with all of them looking around the chair where Julia sat, they still had not been able to locate the missing jewel.

"It's just a little ruby, but it means a lot to me," she said sadly. "It is almost the color of the carpet."

"Wait a minute, I'll go get the flashlight. That'll make it easier for us to see," volunteered Jim.

Quickly he was back with the light in hand. "Here, look how bright it is," he said shining it on the search area of the carpet. After only minutes with everyone on their knees, a shout went up from Joe.

"Here it is," he cried excitedly as he handed it to the now beaming Julia.

"That's really a neat flashlight you have there, Jim. Where did you get it?" asked Tom.

"I found it in the hall closet where we always keep it," said Jim with an odd look at his father.

"Let me see that," Tom said, reaching for the flashlight. "I've never seen this one before. It sure is bright. When did you get this, dear?" he said addressing the question to Anna..

"I didn't buy it, Tom. You must be mistaken. I found it in the attic some time ago." All at once she remembered that she had meant to ask Cook about it. It had completely slipped her mind. Anna could feel all eyes turning on her.

"Well, if it isn't ours, whose is it? How did it get there?"

"I can't imagine, but there has to be a logical explanation. It didn't just get there by itself. I'll check with Cook in the morning."

Cook had already retired and no one felt that the ownership of the flashlight was important enough to disturb her. She had already put in a full day.

That night as Emelia lay in bed, she felt as though she had forgotten something or maybe had left something undone. It left her with a very uneasy feeling that she could not shake.

She could still see her mother's face when she saw the doll. It had the glow of a small child as she had softly spoken, "Min Dukke."

Yes, it had been a truly extraordinary day. In restoring her mother's precious doll they had also revived some of her most wonderful memories. In addition it had also created one of their most memorable moments with Anna.

Finally, Emelia went to sleep from sheer exhaustion, still not sure what it was that she was missing.

What Emelia did not know was that Alfred, indeed, was very interested in the doll. So much so that the next morning he would be gone for the day by six thirty.

Where he would go was never to be shared with any of them, but he was not to return until nearly midnight. If they were to ask where he had been all day, he would, as usual, merely brush it off with, "Just business. Just business."

No one bothered to ask further. First of all, past experience had shown he wouldn't elaborate no matter how much he was asked, and secondly, no one really cared. After all, he was home safe and that was all that counted and his life was his own. Roger and Emelia had more important things to worry about.

In the early morning hours as the others slept, Anna lay wide-awake. Her mind was swimming with so many pleasant childhood memories. I wish my parents were still alive, she thought, as a wave of loneliness swept over her. She found the feeling to be so overwhelming she started to cry.

Tom's stirring next to her brought her back to the present with a start. She reached over and touched his shoulder. Just being next to him always had a calming effect and now was not an exception. She was so lucky to have him and the wonderful family he had given her. How could she be lonely being surrounded with so much love? She supposed it was the stirring of emotions that Emelia had caused that made her think of the past so much lately. It was all connected even if it was so long ago.

It was some time after three that she must have gone to sleep and the next thing she knew it was morning.

Chapter Thirteen

Roger was now convinced that all of the strange events were somehow connected and that they all had something to do with the doll.

First of all, there was the intruder in the night. Where did he, or was it a she, go? The second thought gave him a jolt. The person had obviously gone into the attic. Now if it were a burglar, how many burglars go into people's attics unless they are looking for something specific that would most likely be located there?

Then there was the flashlight found in the attic that no one claimed to have seen before. He had spoken with Cook the morning after Anna's birthday and she denied any knowledge of it.

Then whose was it and how else could it have gotten into the attic where it was found by Anna? It was not in the hall closet the night that Tom had been searching for one when they arrived home to the darkened house.

Once more a cold chill went up his back. The intruder may have been there more than once or twice. The constant nagging thought returned that maybe Emelia was in more danger than any of them realized.

As soon as she returned from her classes that day, she and Roger decided they would try to see if they could decipher anything from the scrap they were guarding. They agreed not to say anything to any of the others because the whole thing seemed so far-fetched.

"It's got to be either serial numbers to something or it is just a bunch of numbers with no meaning at all," she finally said.

They had taken the box that Emelia had come in and tried to make some connection to the numbers, but if there was one, they certainly were not finding it.

Emelia looked over at Roger, who was writing something on a page of white paper going from the scrap and back again. As she watched, she could see the frustration on his face.

"I keep thinking I'm getting something," he said. "Look at this. If you give each one of the numbers a letter equivalent, you get a line of letters. For instance take the letter A and assign it number one, the letter B and assign it number two and then put them together. You'd think you'd come up with something. I'll bet they are not serial numbers at all, but a code to names.

"The first set is 2-8-21-1 which comes out b-h-u-a. Now does that mean anything to you?"

"I'm afraid not," she said. "You don't suppose that the remainder of the code was hidden somewhere else and that both parts are needed to solve the code?"

"That's it! I'll bet that's it! We have half of the puzzle and someone else has the other half. That someone apparently suspects that you have this half, which would explain why you were being chased. They must be quite desperate. What can possibly be so important after all these years that someone would go to such extremes?

"You know," Roger continued, "the more I think about it, I am going to make a copy of this little piece of paper and put the original in the bank box just in case this turns out to be some kind of evidence."

"This is so exciting. I almost wish it would turn out to be some great mystery that we could solve," she said.

"Well, I for one hope that it turns out to be nothing," said Roger. "I don't relish the thought of you, or any of us for that matter, getting hurt."

After some time he said, "You know, I wonder if there is anything at the doll repair shop that would be of help. What if I go there and have a look around?"

"Oh no, I don't want you to take any stupid chances. After all, it may not be anything at all, and why risk ending up in jail for breaking and entering?"

"Well, I didn't plan on getting caught," he said with a smile. "I won't take any chances. I'll make sure that no one is in the house or I won't go in. There isn't any rush except for my curiosity at this point," he ended.

"I'm going with you," she said.

"Oh no, you're not!" he insisted.

"Look, I promise I won't get in the way. I'll stand guard outside while you're inside. It would make me feel like I'm doing something, and besides, I would just be worried sick that something would happen to you if you were there alone. Please?" she pleaded.

Finally she convinced him that if she stayed outside she could go along. He also insisted that they take his father's car because it had a cellular phone and she would be able to call for help if anything went wrong.

That settled, they would begin surveillance of the house and the first night that it was determined to be safe they would put their plan into motion.

For now, Roger would not only copy the little strip with the numbers, but also all of the markings inside and outside of the doll box. Was it possible that these markings might contain the missing clue? This would certainly account for Frieda's intense interest in the box. Maybe even the reason for the chase.

"We aren't taking any chances that we are missing something," he said.

It was on one of the evenings that Roger and Emelia had staked out the "Doll Repair" shop that the theft finally occurred. No one could put a finger on the exact day or time, but Anna was the first to find that the doll box was missing!

"Now we've got to move fast!" It was Roger. "I just feel that there is something very sinister about to happen."

Chapter Thirteen

The stakeout had had one positive result, at least. They had learned that every Sunday evening the occupants of the repair shop left the house at seven p.m. and didn't return until after ten p.m.

"That's three hours. I should be able to get in, search, and get out again in under an hour."

So it was decided on Friday that he would go in on that Sunday.

Neither of them let anyone in on their plans, mainly for two reasons. One, they didn't want interference, good or bad, and two they didn't want to worry Anna or Tom. It was risky, but obviously, to them, so was the future if this mystery remained unsolved.

Meanwhile, another meeting was also taking place. It included a box with numbers and the small piece of "the list."

Every evening Karl would sit and study the list, hoping by doing so he might somehow discover the secret of the code.

So many years had passed and here he was, sure at last the gods had smiled and given the long-awaited chance for revenge. Oh how he hated those whose names must be hidden in those numbers. They just had to find a way to learn their identity. He would arrange a meeting with the others. He needed help and could feel himself getting more and more disappointed and desperate.

It hit him like a bolt of lightning! The reason the numbers and letters didn't make sense was because although they were most likely in sequence, some might be missing.

So it was that they met that night in an open field out of sight.

"I can't believe we've come up with nothing!" It was Otto, the man who had created the replacement leg.

"Let us see what you've got," he said leaning forward so the flashlight hit only the notepad held out to him.

"I've tried everything. Using numbers, using letters for numbers, but nothing comes up.

"See here, I've taken the numbers and put in the corresponding letter, with the number one being A, etc. I come up with c-a-n."

"That can't be it. That's nothing," said the third man.

"I know. That's what I am telling you. There has to be more. I've gone over everything on the box, too, and there's nothing, I tell you."

"There has to be a way. We've come too far to give up now."

"Wait a minute!" It was the youngest of the three. "These were all rich people, right?

"Let's start with that. Who were some of the wealthy aristocrats who lived outside of Germany in the late 1930's who might have been considered targets?"

"Who knows? That's a difficult question because certainly no one would have done this in the open," replied Karl.

"Well, what about anyone whose first name started with C? Let's begin there," said the youngest.

Chapter Fourteen

Anna abruptly lowered her coffee cup as the morning headlines literally jumped out at her.

"Listen to this, Tom." she said as she read. "'Lord Brewster was murdered late last night in the apartment that he shared with his wife. Although Lady Brewster was also shot, she is expected to recover, but she was unable to identify the assailant because he was wearing a ski mask.

"'The apartment security reported to the police that Lord Brewster had received threatening telephone calls, and, as a result, had beefed up their security considerably in the last month. One of their men stated that when Lord Brewster had initially reported the threats, the contents of which he refused to divulge, he seemed very fearful. What those threats were might never be known, but would remain buried with him.

"'Lady Brewster, who is still in a state of shock, was unable to provide details. She will be questioned by the police when the doctors feel that she is able to do so.

"'They are looking into the possibility of blackmail and extortion. They would not comment further, but indicated that evidence may be forthcoming.'

"That poor woman. They were such a lovely couple. They seemed to have everything."

"Maybe a little too much," mused Tom.

Lady Brewster was not asleep, but lay in deep mental anguish with her eyes closed. She could hear all of the activity around her as the busy hospital routine buzzed on. She was going over the events that may have led up to such a terrible ending. Her mind went back to one evening that somehow seemed to hold the clue to what had happened.

Lord and Lady Brewster were getting ready to go to the theater when the telephone rang in the downstairs library.

"Who do you suppose is calling at this time?" asked Estelle. She favored being referred to as Lady Brewster rather than her given name. Only a few close friends were granted permission to use it, and then only in the shortened form of Stella. The form had been started by her father when she was only a child.

"I don't know, but Carrie will get it," said her husband.

Carrie was their maid of 45 years. She probably knew more about them than anyone else on earth. What a book she could write! But then, they would probably outlive her and she would never realize this golden opportunity.

"It's for you, Sir."

Carrie had quickly ascended the stairs and was speaking from outside their door.

"Who is it?" he asked. "See if they can call back later. We are already running behind."

"I tried that, Sir, but he is very persistent. He says it is urgent that he speak with you. He would not take no for an answer."

"Oh, all right. I'll take it in the study." By now curiosity had gotten the better of him anyway. His acquaintances knew him well enough that they wouldn't bother him on a theater night unless they had a very solid reason to do so..

He quickly crossed the room to the study, which was adjacent to their bedrooms on the second floor. He entered, leaving the door slightly ajar. It was very obvious that he didn't appreciate having his schedule interrupted by these commoners who, lord knows, had more time than he did. Emergency indeed!

He sat down and picked up the telephone. At the sound of the voice at the other end he suddenly turned ashen. He had to hold the phone with both hands because they were shaking so severely.

How had the connection been made? What did this person really want?

His mouth was suddenly so dry that he found it difficult even to carry on the short conversation that followed. Before he knew it, the other end of the line went dead and the dial tone was the only audible sound other than the pounding of his heart. He felt it would burst right out of his chest.

The last words kept ringing in his ears over and over. "We know who you really are and what you have done. You are going to pay dearly for it."

Because of her interest in who might be calling, Stella had moved over into the doorway and was listening to his end of the conversation. She was taken aback by the dramatic change in his facial coloring and expression and the severe shaking of his hands.

"What is wrong? Who is it?"

It was as though he were in a trance and it took several seconds for him to recover enough to even acknowledge that she had spoken and entered the room.

He was up and out of the chair, pacing up and down the room like a caged animal. "What do they want from me! What more could they possibly want from me! When is enough enough?"

"What are you talking about?" Stella tried again. Somehow, whatever the call had been, it was obvious that he was deeply disturbed by it. She could not remember ever seeing him so upset. What in the world could the call possibly have been?

But he could not let Stella know. She must never know. It had been so long ago that he had almost managed to forget it. Only on occasion had he even permitted thoughts of it to remotely enter his consciousness. He was not a part of it any longer, or so he had convinced himself until tonight. It seemed like the dead of the past had suddenly been given life again to walk long enough to torment him. Would they kill him? Would they blackmail him? Or would they just be content to terrorize him? What could he possibly do? How could he ever escape them now? He was very famous which he thoroughly enjoyed, and he could never give up this kind of life. But it was also evident that there would be nowhere to hide unless he were willing to sacrifice everything he had worked so long to achieve. No, he just would not do that. He would fight. After all, what good would it all have been for if he just gave up now?

He suddenly stopped and began pounding on the desktop and pushing the papers there onto the floor. This was not just anger, but rage. And yes, there was also something else. That was it! She could see it now in his eyes. It was fear, like that of a cornered wild animal. For the first time in her life, Stella was afraid, not only for him, but for herself as well.

She was talking and had been for some time before he realized that she had been speaking to him.

"What did you say?" he asked, trying again to sound as normal as possible.

"I said, who was the caller? You seem terribly upset by whatever they said."

"Oh, it was just some business," he lied. "I shouldn't let it upset me so."

Actually by now he was once more in full control and had she not seen his reaction Stella would have sworn that there was no need for concern.

However, now thinking back and trying to recall as much as she could of that night she wished she had persisted because, of course, she still had no idea what the substance of the call had been.

"Would you like something for pain?" the nurse was asking. Stella realized that she had been moaning slightly. She wasn't sure if it was from pain or the deep sadness she was feeling at her loss, but she nodded her head yes. It was easier than having to make conversation.

There was something else. She had nearly forgotten about it because it didn't seem at all significant at the time. A short time after the mysterious phone call, her husband had received a letter that he had hurriedly taken into the library to read. He had not emerged for a long time and she thought he was on the telephone talking with someone. She would let the police know when they came again. Maybe the letter was still there in the apartment.

The pain medication had been administered and shortly afterward she fell into a restless sleep.

Chapter Fifteen

During their surveillance, Roger had noted that one of the back windows didn't seem to lock completely and tonight he was grateful that this assessment had been correct. A small tug on the sash and it slid open easily. Within a matter of seconds he was inside. He found himself in total darkness and stood very still for what seemed an eternity before he was able to focus as he made out the shadows of the furniture. The only sound was that of the crickets and other night creatures.

Slowly, he moved over to what looked like a desk. It was then he heard a sound, ever so faint. It was the sound of someone breathing. But it couldn't be! He and Emelia had watched them all leave at seven, right on time as usual.

Then it happened. Something went flying by him and he heard the sound of glass breaking as the object collided with whoever it was.

Roger didn't move. His eyes were now accustomed to the eerie scene. There were two golden eyes looking at him. They were small and close together as though perhaps of a small child. He was frozen, but before he could collect his faculties the intruder moved forward towards him and let out a loud "meow." He nearly collapsed in relief as he realized that the flying object had only been the cat.

I must get hold of myself and get to work, he thought. I have already wasted time. Yes, time was a non-expendable commodity right now.

He was next to what he thought was the desk, but when he turned on his small pen light he realized that it was only a table. After some more maneuvering about, he finally located a desk in one of the bedrooms. There were letters, billing statements, and all sorts of the usual items that one finds in a desk.

After several minutes of not finding anything significant, Roger stopped to take inventory of his options. As he sorted through each drawer he became more and more disappointed. Just as he was pushing in the bottom drawer, he made an interesting discovery. He noted, almost by accident, that the drawer didn't look as deep as it had appeared from the outside. This resulted, with further investigation, in the revelation of a false bottom.

When he was finally able to jostle it open, he nearly jumped back with amazement and disbelief. There was a small portion of what looked like a list of numbers. It was familiar. It looked just like the other portion of what they now referred to only as "the list."

He wanted to snatch it right there and then, but he also knew that its owner would certainly be checking on it sooner or later. If his guess was right, it was more likely sooner. So instead, he took out the small camera he had purchased just for this purpose and began taking pictures of the list. Better take a couple, he thought, just in case one doesn't turn out. He was just getting ready to return the list to its hiding place when he noticed that there was also a letter hidden away.

He realized he should not be snooping around any further. The letter was none of his business and he had already found what he came for. But before he was able to overcome the temptation, he had already convinced himself that because he wasn't taking anything it would do no harm. Ever so carefully he picked up the letter and began to scan it quickly.

He stopped. He read it again, but this time slowly, and then he deliberately placed it on the desk and once again the camera clicked. It was done.

He put everything back into place. All the while his mind was racing like mad. What had he found? What did it mean?

He was unfamiliar with his surroundings and even with the penlight he could easily become disoriented. He must remember how to return to his point of origin.

There was the staircase that Emelia had described, but neither of them had been able to determine the layout of the rooms other than the front area she had seen.

She had certainly been right in her description of it being dusty and cluttered. The stirred-up dust penetrated his nostrils as his movements came in contact with it. There were indeed dolls everywhere. It was really eerie with all those peering eyes. After the experience with the cat, he wouldn't have been surprised if one had jumped out at him. I can't let my imagination interfere with this, he firmly reminded himself.

By his calculations, he still had sufficient time to check the upstairs more thoroughly. Every so often headlights of passing cars illuminated the house. Using the penlight, he decided to continue his search further in case there might be more evidence that would help them solve their puzzle. Upstairs he located nothing unusual in the first two rooms. He was about to enter the third of the upstairs bedrooms when the room suddenly lit up, but this time the lights were not passing. They were coming from the front driveway. He could hear voices just below the window he was standing adjacent to. Someone was coming back much earlier than either he or Emelia had anticipated.

A quick look out the window verified not only that the vehicle was in the driveway, but also that it was the same one that belonged to the owners. He must hurry to get out. He knew that he would have to pass the front door and could only pray that he made it before they did.

He had quickly turned off the penlight, but now that the car lights had been extinguished he found himself in nearly total darkness again. Only when another car passing on the street lit the room for a few seconds was he able to get his bearings. He quickly descended the stairs three at a time, and when he reached the bottom he stumbled over what must have been a stool and fell headlong against a wall. Time was definitely against him now. The slam of one car door, followed by another, indicated that more than one person would soon be at the door. Not only would he be unable to explain his presence, but he could also be charged with forced entry. Not a helpful notation on a law student's resume.

Momentarily stunned, he quickly regained his coordination and began feeling for the penlight he had dropped. Better forget it, he decided as now he heard more distinctly the voices, one a man and the other a woman. He recognized the accent that Emelia had described. His initial hope had been that this might have been a visitor just dropping by, rather than the owners returning home. That hope now completely dissolved.

He was thankful that the camera had been attached to a strap and still hung securely around his neck or he would likely have lost it along with the penlight. Of course, he'd have a bruise where he had fallen on it, but right now that didn't matter.

He was on his feet again and moving toward the back of the house when he heard the key inserted and turn in the lock. No time to waste, he moved forward almost by instinct, praying all the while that he was headed toward the window where he had gained entrance. He was so relieved when he jumped and landed on the grass before the lights came on inside. He didn't worry about closing the window and hoped the owners wouldn't notice. Once safely outside he whispered, "Good night, cat. I am glad you can't talk. Or am I?"

"Over here!" It was Emelia. "We've got to get out of here quick! There is a car that drove in the driveway a couple of minutes ago. The man seemed to be looking for the key, but I know they got in. Did you hear anyone?"

"Yeah, and there's a cat in there that took a couple of years off my life. I mistook him for another night intruder. Let's get out of here!

"Better cut through the back of these other yards and circle back to the car. One thing is for sure, these folks are serious about whatever it is that they are up to."

"What do you mean? Did you find anything?" Emelia was bursting with curiosity.

"Not now, let's hurry before someone catches us here. I'll explain later."

And so it was they were scurrying through one yard after another. They were glad that most of the yards here ran into each other, which made for an open escape route. They were nearly there when all of a sudden Emelia went down. "Oh no!" she cried out. She had slipped on a plastic lid lying on the grass that was already wet with dew.

Lights came on in the house adjacent to where she lay. She clumsily pulled herself back onto her feet and once more made a dash for the street. "There is someone out there," she heard a man yelling. Now a dog began barking wildly as the man opened the door.

Chapter Fifteen

"Come on! " It was Roger who had turned back towards her when he heard her call out. "Are you ok?" There was both urgency and concern in his voice.

"Yes, I am fine, but let's get in the car before that dog decides to come after us." She had just finished saying this when both realized that that was exactly what was happening. Roger pushed her in, then jumped in and slammed the door just before the dog was able to close the gap between them.

Safely inside with the doors locked, they found themselves eye to eye with a large Doberman. He was standing on his hind legs with the front paws resting on the door all the while barking loudly at them.

Roger put the key in the ignition and without turning on the lights drove slowly into the traffic. Only then did he turn on the lights and speed up. He knew he was getting paranoid because there was no way that anyone had followed them.

It wasn't until they were safely back in traffic that either of them relaxed enough to speak.

"I was so afraid for you, Roger," she said hardly breathing.

"It went fine, Sweetie. Wait until you see what I found," he said. He still couldn't put the pieces together.

"We are heading for my place," he said without waiting for her consent and she didn't question his decision.

He thought it best that none of the items be taken to her house where there had been so many unexplained events. Soon he pulled into his driveway and they went in. It felt good to be safe and away from that place.

"Tell me, what did you find?" She couldn't have hidden her excitement had she tried.

"Well, first of all, I found what looks like the match to our list of numbers. I got the pictures and now all we need is to get the film developed. Then, hopefully, we'll be able to figure this out," he said.

"What do you mean, first of all?" she asked.

"Well, I found something else, but it doesn't seem to make much sense right now. It was a letter written to Lord Edward Brewster requesting a donation for something or other. It didn't specify the name of the charity, which it must be, but it sounded different, almost threatening in tone."

"What do you mean threatening? I'm sure that these large charities can get somewhat ruthless now and then when they run low on funds and probably put the strong arm on some of their contributors who have a tendency to become a little lax in giving."

"No, it didn't sound like that. Oh, I forgot to mention that I found both of these items well hidden in a false bottom drawer. Why would anyone put a request for a contribution in a hiding place and why would these people be connected with some meaningful charity?"

"I see what you mean," she said slowly, turning to face him. "What exactly did it say?"

"I took a picture of it also, so as soon as it is developed we can study it. It may have a logical explanation. Or it may have no connection with this whole thing."

Chapter Fifteen

"Oh, Roger, I am so glad we don't have to go back to that awful place again." She snuggled up close to him and he put his arm around her shoulder.

"Me, too," he said and he really meant it. He thought about how very frightened he had been when the cat had startled him, but he would not embellish that part of the adventure when he would later relate the story to the others.

"Let's keep this a secret until we are sure what we have," he said.

"The fewer people who know about this for now, the better," she quickly added.

"You know, Emelia, tonight I suddenly realized how much you mean to me. Come here," he said softly. He gently cupped her face in his hands. He leaned forward and she closed her eyes knowing that he was going to kiss her. Her arms went around his neck as he pulled her close to him. She felt so very happy and safe.

He held her thus for a long time, not wanting to let her or this moment go.

It was early afternoon the following day when Roger was able to arrange for the film to be developed. He had chosen a friend whose hobby was photography to do it for him. He didn't want the film out of his control nor did he want to wait for its return with the possibility of it getting lost. It had taken too much effort to obtain the pictures to get careless at this stage of the game. The friend had not required any explanation and was more interested in the quality of the pictures than the content.

He knew Roger well enough to respect his desire for confidentiality. The pictures were soon developed and the two shared a soda and some small talk as they waited for them to dry.

In half an hour Emelia would be arriving at Roger's apartment. They had made arrangements earlier in the day to meet in order to study their "evidence."

Within an hour, they had everything laid out on his dining room table. It consisted of the list that had been in the wig dome, the copy of the letters taken from the doll box that Roger had saved early on, the picture of the list confiscated from the repair shop, and finally the picture of "the letter."

"Let's see what we can learn about the lists."

So he took their original list and, as before, substituted the letters for numbers. They had the b-h-u-a. Now doing the same with the other list, they got c-a-n.

"That doesn't make any more sense than before," she said.

"Just be patient, Sweetie," he said. "Let's try to put them together."

He tried putting them one after the other, backwards, but nothing came of that.

"Wait! Whoopee! I've got it!" he shouted at the same time jumping to his feet.

"Look, here. Take our letters b-h-u-a and insert their c-a-n and what do you see? B-c-h-a-u-n-a. Now take the b and use it as the first initial. B. Chauna. Aha!" he said proudly.

"The only B. Chauna I know of is Benjamin Chauna, the father of Charlene Chauna, the Cosmetic Queen," said Emelia.

"Could be," he replied. "Let's try the next one. Our list is 6-8-12-14 or f-h-l-n."

"This one is 5-18-9-7 or e-r-i-g which we could make f-e-h-r-l-i-n-g," said Emelia. "That makes F. Ehrling, another wealthy individual. There is a Sir Frank Ehrling, founder of the multimillion dollar Ehrling Enterprises!"

"This is very interesting." He interjected. "Next, our list is 5-18-23-20-18 or e-r-w-t-r. This list is 2-5-19-5 or b-e-s-e. Let me put those together and we get E. Brewster."

"What did you say? E. Brewster, that's got to be Edward Brewster. Lord Brewster! He was just murdered a couple days ago! Can it be connected to this?" she asked in disbelief.

"It might be that someone else has successfully broken the code already. If murder is the result, what is the motive? We have to move fast before someone else gets hurt," Roger said. He then added, "Wait a minute. Let me see the picture of the letter. I think it was addressed to Lord Brewster!"

It took a magnifying glass, but Roger could easily make out the text because he had already seen the copy in the repair shop.

"What does it say?" asked Emelia.

"'Because you have chosen to ignore my telephone calls, I feel it necessary to remind you that your contribution is overdue. Unless this is received by Friday at five p.m. you will be dropped. Do you fully understand how serious the results would be? I hope so.'"

There was no signature.

"Do you think these contributions, or more likely lack thereof, could be the reason he was killed? What shall we do?" she asked.

"We have to figure out a way to get the facts to the police before someone else gets killed. This information is too dangerous, but they'll know what to do."

"What do you mean, figure out a way?" she asked. "Why can't we just go and give it to them?"

"Well, Sweetie, there's just one small problem called forced entry, which, to put it mildly, is a crime. I have no intention of destroying my career, much less going to jail," he said.

"Oh, that's right. With all the excitement I guess I forgot that angle. So what can we do?" she asked.

"I've given this a lot of thought since we set up our little breaking and entering scheme. The way I see it we can use the protected attorney-client privilege here."

"Now you've lost me. You're not an attorney, at least, not yet," she countered.

"No, I'm not." He now laughed, seeing her skepticism. "But Simon Goldstein, our family attorney, can provide the link. I'll give him what we've got and he can to go the police with it. Our conversation is considered privileged and he isn't required to reveal his sources, namely you and me."

"What a coincidence! Simon and Irene have been friends of my family for years. That's a wonderful idea, Roger," she said as she gave him a spontaneous hug. But then she suddenly stopped. "What if he doesn't agree?"

"Oh, I think he will once he hears what we have. It's even more likely since he knows us both that he'll help."

Even though it was already evening they made the decision not to wait until the next day. A hasty phone call to the attorney's home with just enough information to whet his curiosity gleaned the anticipated results. And soon they were on their way to see him.

Simon Goldstein personally met them at the door, reinforcing that he was indeed interested to learn the facts of their story. For the next couple of hours Roger and Emelia laid out for him what they knew and what they suspected.

He listened and interrupted only when clarification of some minor point was needed. It didn't take long to establish that they had found the one person who would protect their identity and still pass on the information to the police.

Once the visit had accomplished its goal, Emelia and Roger prepared to leave, with the agreement that each would be kept informed as the wheels were set into motion.

"I do have to say you have done a great job with your detective work, but I need to warn you that breaking and entering could have had serious ramifications.

Not only from the standpoint of the law, but also the danger of an encounter with the owners of the repair shop. I want you to promise that you won't try that again," Simon said in a fatherly tone.

"Don't worry," they both said in unison.

"Once is enough," added Roger. "I don't know when I've been so scared." This time it didn't seem important that Emelia knew.

"Good. I'll go to the police first thing in the morning. The sooner they get this the better."

The police were more than a little interested, especially since the list included the name of the deceased Lord Brewster, and they were already in possession of the original letter.

The following day there would indeed be more evidence forthcoming, as the police had predicted.

Chapter Sixteen

It was late afternoon the following day by the time Roger arrived for supper at the Hansen house. He had spent the better part of the day back at the police station, trying to learn as much as possible.

It had been a very exhausting day. The family was eagerly awaiting an update. They had heard rumors that Aunt Joanna had been arrested and that Uncle Frederick had been hospitalized with a heart attack as a result.

"What's going on, Roger?" Tom was the first one to the door. "Come in. You can fill us in while we eat."

"That sounds like an invitation. I'm starved. I've been too busy to eat."

When everyone was finally seated, which included Aunt Julia, but not Uncle Alfred, who was again off on business, Roger began.

"It's really all very simple now, looking back. When I ran into your Aunt Joanna about a week ago, she made a comment about your doll, Anna. She said she hoped you'd be pleased with your birthday gift and wished she could see your face when you saw the doll. It wasn't until later that I remembered that she had not been included in the plan. So how could she know? Only you, Tom, Emelia and myself outside of the repair shop would have had any knowledge of the repair, to say nothing of the doll itself.

"The more I thought about it, the more suspicious I became. I still couldn't put her together with it so decided not to mention anything lest I was making some wrong assumptions.

"Then yesterday, after Simon took our information to the police, they immediately began to put two and two together. They went with a search warrant to the repair shop, where they located, among other things, the letter I had copied. Once they had it, they brought Frieda and Karl in for questioning. It was Frieda who broke first and implicated Joanna as one of them.

"Anyway, today I learned more about Joanna than I guess any of you were aware. She is really half Jewish, which accounts for a large portion of this story.

"She was able to conceal this because her mother, who was a Jew, died when Joanna was born and her father, who remarried within a year, was not. It was thought best to keep this secret, since Hitler made his hatred of the Jews a well-known fact.

"As a result, Joanna didn't know this until one night after her return from a date with a Gestapo officer. Her father was so incensed that he told her of her heritage and the danger that she could be in if anyone found out.

So terrified was Joanna that she even stopped dating altogether for nearly a year.

"During that time, she tried to find out as much about her heritage as possible without letting those around her know. Her curiosity, which was insatiable, led her to the discovery of the 'trains' and the gas chambers. She was so horrified that she decided to join the underground to help those less fortunate than herself to escape any way they could."

Anna found it difficult to sit still and walked over to stand next to Tom. She wondered how, even though she had known Joanna all of her life, it was possible that she didn't really know much about her at all, at least not her earlier life. This person was a stranger and it amazed her that so much had been omitted.

Roger, noting her restlessness, said, "I'm sure this is all very disturbing to you, but maybe you should sit down. It gets worse, much worse."

At that Tom took her hand and gently pulled her down to sit next to him as Roger continued.

"Joanna was soon deeply involved. She learned what to look for and how the Gestapo worked. She was constantly aware that there were spies everywhere, including in the underground, whose goal it was to capture not only those trying to escape, but also those assisting them. As one of the latter she was playing a very dangerous role. The longer she remained with the underground the greater the master of this cat and mouse game she became. In fact, the satisfaction she felt each time a successful escape was pulled off brought on a new and more exhilarating high.

"It was during this time that she met a young Dutchman, Peter, who was as committed as she to helping these people. It was he who told her about the group of wealthy and elite contributors from the outside who supported not only the philosophy but also the activities of the Reich. Once the idea of the Master Race was accepted all over the world, these elite would be highly celebrated and honored, which made the present dilemma bearable. However, at that time, the world would have been astounded by the identity of these prominent outsiders. Had their identity been known, they would most likely have faced financial ruin. It turns out that their names were only known by a couple of the highest-ranking Gestapo officers and these contributors would remain secret even from one another.

"Only one list, the one in the hands of the Gestapo, was purported to exist. It was used originally only to identify the contributors, but it had also become useful to the Reich to continue sucking more and more money from those whose allegiance had begun to shift as the war dragged on. The Reich needed funds and knew the quickest and, unfortunately, often the most cruel way to get what they wanted.

"Their main goal, however, was to finance the spy movement so as to prevent or stop the escape routes to safety. Many innocent men, women and children never escaped, but died either where they were stopped or were sent away to suffer atrocities in the concentration camps." He stopped for a breath. It was interesting, but long ago.

It was then that Tom, with a puzzled look, said, "Before you go on, Roger, I've got to ask this. How were you able to get all this information? My understanding has always been that the police are very tight-lipped, particularly when they are in the investigative phase."

"You're right about that! If it hadn't been for Simon letting me tag along, I wouldn't have learned any of this. Because he had given them our information, they included him more than they normally do. He is also a personal friend of the police chief, but I don't know if that made any difference. By the way, he is planning to stop here a little later. He was talking with Alfred when I left.

"Anyway, to your question regarding yours truly. Simon introduced me merely as a law student, a friend of the family, spending time with him to get hands-on experience for a class. I'm sure that no one suspects that I'm one of the sources. You know, he's really a terrific guy."

"Okay, so you're at the station in the eye of the storm, so to speak. So now that that's cleared up, go on," Tom said.

"Before you do," Emelia interrupted, "I don't understand what any of this has to do with our list."

"Don't you see? Those giving money to the Reich helped to prolong the time that they remained in power. To the victims of that power and their families who suffered so horribly under them, these were monstrous traitors with no decency.

"Because of the danger of their ugly role it was important to the Reich, who wanted to continue to benefit from their services, that their identity remain secret, even from one another.

"However, one day the list disappeared and several men who were suspected of the plot to steal it were immediately executed. Unfortunately for the Gestapo, or for that matter those named in the list, in their haste to punish they had foolishly overlooked the fact that with the death of these men they may have lost any chance of its recovery. Over the years many stories and rumors concerning the list had sprung up, including that it had been burned or ended up in a convent. Some had even speculated that it had been put into various articles and spirited out of the country.

"In spite of the stories, nothing concrete had ever surfaced. Meanwhile, those on the list had been lulled into a false security, sure that it had been destroyed in the rubble when the war finally ended. They were confident that their ties to the Reich and its philosophy would remain undetectable because so much time had passed. Certainly, because it had been in code, even if it were found it wouldn't have been recognized as anything other than trash."

"That does make sense, but what does this have to do with Aunt Joanna?" Tom asked.

"Well, that's the part that is sad and shows what hate can do to a person. Peter and Joanna had decided that they wanted to get married and that the war would probably go on for some time. So they made arrangements to be married on Christmas Eve in 1938. They were so excited and happy that they didn't notice that they were being followed. Just after they had exchanged their vows and were coming out of the church, Peter was gunned down right in front of Joanna's eyes."

"Oh, how dreadful!" cried Emelia as she covered her face with both hands. "What did she do then?"

"I really couldn't learn any details because apparently there isn't anyone now alive who was there."

"Then how did you learn all of this?" Anna asked before he could resume.

"That was another benefit of being with Simon. We had the chance to observe some of the questioning from the observation booth just adjacent to them. It had the glass, you know, where we could see them, but on the other side they see only a mirror."

"Oh, wow!" said one of the twins.

"Anyway, as to how I learned this much. Part was Frieda's version when she was questioned and part was Joanna's. Frieda is the lady of the repair shop," he said looking at Emelia. "She was actually the source of the details of most of Joanna's past.

"It seems that the two women met during the war and became close friends. Joanna was responsible for getting Frieda's parents to safety, but failed when it came to her brother. Apparently, Frieda never held that against her.

"Watching Joanna was something else. It seemed almost like a catharsis for her to tell her story. I'll tell you, watching her gave me the creeps. At times it seemed as though she was looking right at me, but, of course, I knew she couldn't be. She had no idea who was on the other side of the glass, but you can bet that she knew she was being watched. She made that clear by looking directly into the glass when making some specific point. She's a cold one.

"I think learning of Joanna's background and the tragedy of Peter's death will perhaps help you to understand what has happened since."

He stopped and took a drink of water from the glass that Anna had set down in front of him. Everyone's attention was so focused that had a pin dropped it would have been heard.

"Joanna was so shattered and eventually so full of hate that she set out to learn what she could about the elite and wealthy that Peter had told her about. If she could just learn the name of even one, she would find him or her and seek revenge for Peter's death. Unfortunately for Lord Brewster, even after so many years had passed, it was his name that she discovered. She set out to blackmail him. But when the extortion failed, she set out to terrify him into paying. Instead, she ended up killing him. It was she who was in the ski mask in the Brewster's apartment that Lady Brewster could not identify."

"It can't be!" Anna was on her feet. "I have known Joanna for years. She may be an irritating person, but blackmail and murder? She couldn't!"

"I am just as shocked and sad as you are, but if you check, you will find that she was not only questioned, but also arrested. She confessed to the police just a little over an hour ago."

"But how did she find out Lord Brewster was on the list?" asked Emelia.

"That really happened by accident, too. While we have been involved trying to solve the mystery of the doll, other meetings were also taking place," continued Roger.

"Because you see, Emelia, by now the woman in the repair shop, Frieda, and her husband, Karl, had recognized the doll. They knew all about the list of names that had been put into a doll's leg—a doll just like this one—a German edition Armand Marseille. When they noticed the cracked leg, even though they could hardly believe their luck, they felt that it might be the long-lost doll, and, in fact, it turned out that it was. They wanted those names badly.

"The plan was to extort as much money as possible from these traitors without ever revealing their own identity. Once that was done, they would turn them over to an Israeli court. The harsh punishment they would surely receive would make their lives a living nightmare.

"Yes, we leaned that, too. Frieda and Karl had also worked in the underground and had seen so many of their friends and relatives killed because of the spies. They knew that there were wealthy contributors who paid the spies well. These same spies were the ones who infiltrated their ranks to accomplish their dirty work and annihilate the innocent.

"They knew that there was a list and that the story of the doll was true."

"I think someone just drove up," said Cook, who was preparing to serve the main course.

"That's probably Simon," said Roger, holding onto his still untouched salad as Cook began collecting plates.

She gave him a big smile. "Don't worry, I'll let you eat it while you stop for a breath." No one worried about her presence during family conversations. If anyone could be trusted to maintain a confidence, it was Cook.

Just then the doorbell rang.

"I'll get that," said Tom, already out of his chair and halfway to the door.

"Hi, Simon. Come in. Roger thought it might be you."

"Yes, I did mention that I might drop by. I wanted to see how everyone is bearing up and if there are any questions that I might be able to answer. I'm sure Roger has filled you in on most of it already. It's been quite a day!"

Simon Goldstein was nearly the same height as Tom. He was a much older man, but because he was so active and interesting, people tended to forget his age. He had the appearance that goes with being the very successful man that he was. He walked as straight and dignified as he had in his twenties when he graduated at the top of his class from law school. His blue eyes hadn't lost any of their sparkle, which only enhanced his sense of humor. One that was always there just below the surface.

He had been talking about retirement for at least the last ten years, but still his practice gave no indication that it would take place any time in the near future.

He had really enjoyed Roger's company and was secretly toying with the idea of engaging him in his practice if he turned out to be as sharp as he seemed to demonstrate. He had always longed for a son to carry on what he had begun, but fate had ruled otherwise. He decided he was going to keep his eyes on this one. Perhaps now he had found a substitute.

"Why don't you join us, Simon?" said Anna as Tom moved another chair to the table.

"Oh, I didn't come by to eat," he offered in mild protest.

"There's plenty. I'll get another plate," said Cook as she vanished into the kitchen before he could refuse. She thought of him and his wife, Irene, as friends of the family. They had been coming to the house for as long as she could remember. Most of those visits had been just that. Business was handled at the office.

"I'd call Irene, but she's visiting her sister this evening. I left a message that I was coming here so if she needs me she'll find me."

Now that the small talk was over each again began concentrating on the delicious meal.

"This is fantastic," said Simon as Cook placed the plate in front of him. "I knew there had to be a reason I came directly here without stopping for a burger."

Cook laughed. She loved cooking, but loved even more the raves she received as a reward for her efforts.

"Roger has been telling us about your exciting day and how you took him under wing. We really appreciate everything you're doing," finished Tom.

"Well, my boy," Simon said, looking at Roger. "You left before all the commotion was over."

"I saw you talking to Alfred. What did he have to say?"

"Are you ready for another shocker?" he said and paused for a moment.

Forks and spoons stopped between plates and mouths as questioning eyes turned on him.

"What do any of you really know about your Uncle Alfred? What he does or even where he goes?" His words just hung there in midair. No one spoke because in truth they didn't have the answers.

"What do you mean, what he does?" asked Anna with alarm.

"I spent a lot of time with him this evening. He was very open with me. Maybe it's because I look trustworthy or he just needed to talk. He is a very, very interesting man.

"His true identity goes way back prior to the war years. As a young man, he willingly embarked on a sinister, lonely career as a spy for the resistance movement. This fact was never revealed to even those closest to him.

"He was one of few foreigners residing in Germany who to all outward appearances expressed no opinion regarding either side in the pending war and showed no concern for the politics swirling around him.

"The handsome, charming, womanizing personality had been meticulously practiced and perfected to mask the double life he had undertaken. Added to that, born with the proverbial silver spoon, his wealth allowed him to travel freely in and out of Germany without question.

"As a result he became one of the most valuable agents for the Allies because he was able not only to obtain vital information in advance and memorize it, but also to bring it out safely on his own.

"Don't get me wrong," Simon interjected. "He knew he was in danger of discovery at any time. He said he learned to live with that fear, and even though he had recurring nightmares and frequently woke at night in a cold sweat he didn't stop doing what he saw as his destiny.

"In fact, he was instrumental in learning the name of the intended doll recipient from a German informant, but had no way of knowing that the doll had been switched. It was his assignment to get the list so that the contributors could be made known and the flow of money into the Reich would cease.

"The most mysterious part of all was that the switch was successful, which is why it could never be traced, nor the list confiscated.

"He arranged for a car that killed the German spy who came to intercept the doll in England. The original plan had been that he would confront the man and get the doll from him, feigning that he was to be his contact with the contributors. Once he had done that, the man would have to be killed before he could report back to his superiors because they would then realize that they had been duped. Also Alfred's cover would have been blown. Therefore, he had no real choice in the situation. When the doll turned out to be the wrong one—because, of course, we now know that Emelia was the right one—the wheels had already been set in motion for the kill and Alfred was helpless to stop them. He did emphasize to me that killing the spy, however, had been of no deep concern to him. He would have liked to get as many of them as he could. If it hadn't been for them, his father might still be alive. Tragically he had been discovered hiding a Jewish friend and as a result both were executed on the spot.

"Although the doll was lost and the war over, Alfred's mission did not stop there. All those trips that you envied were actually assignments coordinated with his superiors to track down war criminals who had escaped justice.

"Again, Alfred's wealth provided the perfect cover for a gentleman who loved to travel and didn't have to worry about the expense. These trips took him all over the world, most of the time with little success, to areas including Argentina, Brazil and Australia. You name it. The worst part, according to him, was the mundane travel books that he was forced to co-author to add to his cover. He did admit, however, that this gave him some recognition in social circles, an area that he has never neglected.

"It wasn't until you took the doll to the repair shop, talk about coincidence, that the lost doll would again fall into the hands of someone who not only knew what this meant, but whose hatred and search for vengeance was as alive as the day the doll had disappeared.

"The reason Alfred arranged to stay with you now was because of a tip from his superiors that the long-lost list may have been found in this area. He still had no idea that the doll had any connection to you. And who could imagine the likelihood of Alfred, who is not even a relative, ending up in the same household as the very doll for which he had killed so many years before? Talk about a small world."

"What is going to happen to Uncle Alfred?" asked Emelia with concern.

"Yeah? I don't want anything bad to happen to him," said Joe, his eyes filled with tears.

"Me neither," echoed Jim, caught up in his brother's concern. "I love Uncle Alfred."

For two little boys who rarely sat still for any length of time, much less listened, they had been absolutely riveted to their seats as the story unfolded. So quiet had they been that their presence had been all but forgotten.

Simon now turned to them and in a reassuring voice said, "I'm sure nothing is going to happen to your Uncle Alfred."

Then, including the others again, he continued, "For one thing, the only death in which he was involved regarding this whole issue was that of the German spy. He would probably have gotten a medal had he been able to complete his assignment and intercept the real doll. After all, his idea of revenge was to be able to expose those on the list for what they were: traitors. Murder and blackmail were never part of his agenda."

"Where is he now? Do you know?" asked Tom.

"I left him at the police station, where he has been trying to help them put the pieces together. After all, he's on their side."

"That was the business to which he referred when we wondered where he was spending so much time," said Emelia.

"He did tell me that after this is over, he is officially retired and plans to take a long vacation," said Simon.

"I'll bet he doesn't plan on any traveling in the near future," finished Roger.

"This is all so unbelievable. To think that my Emelia held the secret all those years," said Anna.

"And would have continued to do so if we hadn't decided on her restoration," said Tom.

Roger once again took up the tale. "When the doll was dropped off for repair, Karl called his friend Hans, your gardener. They enlisted his son, Rudy, who was the one who broke into the house the first time to try to find the doll box, thinking that it held the clue. He was also the one who caused the door to slam the night the lights were off. Remember, Tom, you thought it was due to the wind.

"It was his flashlight that you saw, Aunt Julia, thinking the family had not gone to the theater. You were also right about the time when you insisted that it had been before we arrived back here around eleven. I checked with Cook and she said that she, too, saw what she thought was a flashlight that night. She convinced herself that it was probably only a reflection that you had both seen."

"What next?" asked Tom. "Boy, you gentlemen have certainly been busy detectives."

"Emelia, remember how you said something about Rudy acting strange in class? Was it the day after we had gone to the theater?"

"Why, yes it was. Well, that explains it. How many times was he in the house? I can't believe it."

"Oh, my goodness," said Anna holding her hands up to her face. "It must have been Rudy who placed the telephone calls when no one answered. He was staking out the house trying to see if it was empty. His first attempt apparently failed when we came home from the theater and interrupted him. That's when he dropped the flashlight. That's why you didn't recognize it, Tom. It belonged to Rudy."

"See, Jim and I weren't the ones who messed up your attic. We told you so, Mom," Joe said, now in much better spirits.

"Yes, I am sorry that I blamed you," she said while smiling at them.

"Rudy obviously didn't find the box on that occasion because it was not in the attic," said Roger, "but in your closet. So he had to come back again. Because you see, Emelia, by now Frieda and Karl had recognized the doll and had taken the partial list out of the leg.

"Yes, I learned that, too. It had been put into the leg by the Gestapo and was intended to go to London. Their agent was to intercept it and contact the contributors to get more money from them, either willingly or by blackmail. However, as I mentioned before, the wrong doll was sent and its recipient, whose identity Alfred had learned, was killed.

"Anyway, back to the story. Hans called the doll repairman, Otto, who had worked in the original factory in Germany. He is the one who made a new leg for the doll after they destroyed the original in order to get the list out. But to their dismay, a part of the list was still missing. That's the part that we still had that you found in the wig dome, Emelia," he said looking at her.

"They thought that the box might hold the clue and when Frieda saw the numbers and letters on the cleaned-up box she was determined that the answer lay in it.

"So they set upon the plan to get it away from you when they chased your car. They had already made several tries. First when Rudy came to the house twice then the last attempt that was made by Hans."

"That must have been when I came home and found him on the stairs!" exclaimed Anna. "He was not ill, but pale with fright that he had been caught in the house and afraid that he might have been seen upstairs. I can't believe I could have been so stupid. Still, they didn't get the box."

"You're not stupid, dear. Just trusting," said Tom. "And that's not a flaw."

"But you still haven't told us how Joanna found out who was on the list, much less how the others did," said Tom.

"Well, as I see it, the six of them somehow stumbled across the first three names. And I mean stumbled because they never did have the remainder of the code. You did, Emelia. But they had guessed at the first two initials and were somehow able to hit pay dirt: Edward Brewster, F. Ehrling and B. Chauna. Of course, Benjamin Chauna was already deceased so they zeroed in on the daughter, Charlene. Because of her close relationship with her father she was fully aware of his earlier alliance with the Third Reich. A little telephone call to each was all that it took. The shock took them all off balance, which gave them away."

"We know there was Hans, Karl, Rudy, Otto and Frieda, so that must make Joanna number six," said Aunt Julia, who had not spoken a word until now. She was in a complete daze.

"Precisely!"

"Apparently the night after the doll was left at the shop, there was a meeting of the original four, one of whom was Joanna. The other three were Karl, Hans and Otto. Joanna was dressed as a man. Remember, she had to learn all about disguises in her days in the underground, so she had no problems doing so on this and other occasions."

"Oh, poor Uncle Frederick. What did he say? Does he know?" Anna asked.

"Yes, he was by her side. In a state of shock, I might say. He still doesn't know the whole story and probably never will.

"After she confessed, he complained of chest pain and police called for an ambulance. I doubt he ever did know about Peter and Joanna's secret life. The fact that she was in love with another man all these years will be a hard pill for him to swallow," ended Roger.

Chapter Seventeen

Uncle Frederick died early the next morning and thus was spared the agony of the drama that was soon to consume what was left of Joanna's life.

Her love for Peter would remain forever concealed from him, and for that she was grateful. Although she did not experience the romantic kind of love that she had felt with Peter, she had cared deeply for Frederick. He had always been there, a quiet and trustworthy man who had kept his marriage vows "till death do us part."

She would miss him, but it was Peter that dominated her thoughts now. Even though she had only partially succeeded, she felt that he would have been pleased with her act of revenge.

No, she would never be sorry! The retribution on Peter's behalf was worth going to prison. Even for the remainder of her life, if that was the price. She had lost her real life, the one with Peter, years ago.

"Things will never be the same again," said Emelia with distinct sadness in her voice.

"No," agreed Anna. "I wonder how much would have stayed the same had Emelia, with her concealed mystery, remained in the attic?"

"We'll never know that, but life takes its little detours now and then and apparently this was one of them. Emelia's appointment with destiny is over. She kept her secret for as long as needed and now she can spend the rest of her days dressed in her finery and being admired," said Tom.

"What is going to happen to the others? How many on the list had they been able to contact and extort, or attempt to extort?" asked Emelia, turning to Roger.

"I guess we will learn more about that after the police finish their investigation and the trial gets under way. I, for one, want to forget all of this for the present and just get back to a humdrum life for a while," said Roger.

What Roger really wanted was to be alone with Emelia and take her in his arms and tell her how much he loved her. He had played the scene over and over in his mind the last couple of days. When would he tell her?

It would be tonight. He could not endure another sleepless night even though putting the plan into action could be risky. She was not a girl that you said "I love you" to and then expected to hop into bed. Oh no, it was a lifetime commitment that he wanted and he wanted it badly.

This was an emotion that he had never felt before and he had to be sure that she felt the same.

"How about we take in a movie, Emelia, and just relax for a while?" he asked.

Once agreed, with Anna and Tom's blessing, they were off.

"I'm glad you suggested a movie, Roger. I really do need to think about something other that the events of the last few weeks. It's been exhausting," she said.

"We don't need to go to a movie, you know. I really just used that as an excuse to get you alone. Do you mind if we drive out by the lake and just sit and talk?"

"No, it seems like a long time since we have been able to concentrate on anything but our mystery," she finished.

He swung the car around and headed for the lake that was only about a mile away. Neither spoke as they traveled along the now almost deserted road that lay in shadows as the moon danced in and out of the trees. Suddenly, they were there. The moon, like a suspended lantern, reflected off the mirror-like surface of the lake.

The scene was perfect, he thought: the moon, the lake, but best of all, the right girl. He could feel the small box in his pocket and hoped that the ring would be on her finger before they left this spot. He could feel not only the excitement, but also that his courage had now returned and he felt in full control. Yes, she would be his.

"What are you thinking, Roger?" she asked.

“I need to be honest with you, Emelia. My feelings for you have changed over the past few weeks,” he began.

“Oh,” she said in almost a whisper, as she felt a sense of panic. He is going to dump me, she thought. I have misunderstood his intentions. Didn’t his own mother tell me that he never gets serious about anyone? She could hear her own words to Anna, “It’s not like I am going to marry him. We’re only friends.”

She could feel her eyes beginning to sting as she fought back the tears. No matter what, she would remain in control. She would not let him see her cry.

“Please look at me, Emelia,” he said. She had turned her head away from him and was looking out the window while regaining her composure.

I am just going to die, she thought, but turned and faced him anyway.

He immediately sensed a change in her. Did she know what he was going to ask and was avoiding looking at him because she didn’t want to hurt him? He wasn’t going to stop now.

“Emelia, we mean a lot to each other. We have spent a lot of time together and I don’t think I could ever live without you. I need you and I want you so much,” he let the words just tumble out.

“Oh, Roger,” she said as she threw herself into his arms. “I want you, too.”

“Just a minute,” he said as he reached into the little box and held out the diamond ring he had so painstakingly picked out and said, "Will you marry me, Emelia?"

By now, she was smiling and crying at the same time. "Oh, yes, Roger, I will marry you. I love you so much."

He slipped the ring on her finger, pulled her to him and kissed her long and hard.

"You are going to laugh at me," she continued. "When you said your feelings had changed, I thought you were getting ready to dump me."

"What! How could you possibly think that? Me, the kind and caring all-around good guy?" he teased. "My love for you will never change. I want for us to have the kind of love that your mother and father have, and we will."

They would not yet make love; there would be the wedding night for that, but for now they were content to just be close and share their lovers' kisses.

He turned to her and murmured ever so softly, "Min Dukke."

Acknowledgments

Many thanks to my parents, whose love and beliefs provided the stability and space for me to develop my God-given talents; my brother, Ove Jensen, whose support, I never doubted; my dear friend, Susan Gallego, who assisted with reading and re-reading as the chapters slowly emerged; my daughters, Ingrid and Heidi, for the understanding of their mother's desire to achieve as an author; and my editor, Lisa Tawney, whose skill and patience cannot be overemphasized.

About the Author

Ellen Jensen-Dean, one of two children of Danish immigrants, grew up on a farm in southern Minnesota.

It was on her one and only trip to Denmark at the age of five that she received the Armand Marseille doll, a Christmas present from her grandparents, which would later offer the inspiration for her mystery, *En Dukke.* Although the details are fictional, the eruption of World War II and Hitler's reign furnished a pivotal point for the story.

Upon graduation from the Fairview Hospital School of Nursing in Minneapolis and obtaining her RN, Ellen headed west to California to practice her chosen profession of nursing.

Even though nursing and family occupied much of her time, she never lost sight of a lifelong dream to become an author. With many of her experiences, including life-and-death events, she has a wealth of information to draw upon.

She currently resides in Southern California with her family and considers this home.